THE REMF RET̶U̶R̶NS

PRAISE FOR THE REMF RETURNS

"The REMF is back, and those who enjoy Vietnam novels will welcome him. Willson's unnamed diarist is in the real army, not Rambo's army. Every soldier knows the REMF— the rear echelon clerk who whines rather than fights and dodges duties instead of bullets. He is the guy who promoted a good deal for himself. Willson's man has an accurate eye for the details of military and Vietnamese life in and around Saigon in 1967. He protects himself and entertains the reader with intelligence and humor."

John Newman, Curator
Vietnam War Literature Collection
Colorado State University

"For every infantry soldier who was actually fighting in Vietnam, there were at least five to six other rear-area personnel to support him. After all, soldiers have to be processed in, fed, housed, supplied and resupplied, medically looked after, counselled (spiritually and legally), paid, entertained, and damn near anything and everything else by someone else in uniform to keep the war rolling.

"These rear-area soldiers were known as REMFs; which meant they were Rear Echelon Mother Fu . . . . eh, you get the point. Their fight was often against such enemies as boredom, tedium, petty bureaucracy, and the many absurdities that made up the other side of the war.

"*REMF Diary* and *The REMF Returns* are well calculated and crafted looks at the other Vietnam; the kind where Willson's subtle and biting humor makes you think long after he makes you laugh!"

Kregg P.J. Jorgenson, author of
Acceptable Loss: an Infantryman's
Perspective of Vietnam, and
Inches to Live, Seconds to Die

"Dear David,

"I liked your continuing saga *The REMF Returns*, particularly the ending—or the intermission, if there's a third volume to be. Its time-capsule dimension had me daydreaming away of old books, movies, rock songs of the time ('House of the Rising Sun' must have played 100 times x week, plus 'We Gotta Get Out of This Place'), beginning on the second page with your reference to AFRTS; the first night I hit the EM club under the old camouflage parachute at Saigon Support Command, AFRTS was on, and the DJ identified himself as 'Army Specialist Don L. Brink,' and I fell into a trance, Don Brink being the WIBG guy I listened to for hours riding up and down between NY and Philadelphia in the early 60's to visit a friend in school there. One quality everybody remembers about Vietnam: things kept collapsing into other things. Whose movie are we in? Or, *TZ*-style, dum-de-dum-de, dum-de-dum-de. Was it a Lenny Bruce routine where he went, 'oo-EEE-ooo,' the SF horror-film audio signal that strange things are about to happen? Anyway. Liked little touches about the officers and gentlemen (one of hardest realizations for me to get through my head was 'officers are people too,' never did get the hang of it), liked all the stuff with Dead Head Ed. Noted that we read a lot of the same books."

Robert Chatain, author of
The Ant War

"Yes, the psychic double cousin of Stonewall Jackson and Andy Warhol served time in Vietnam; this is his second book on the war. He passed his day listening to 'Leopard Skin Pill Box Hat' and other hits of the era. A hard-fought war indeed for those stationed behind the lines in places like Long Binh Junction. The lifers vs. the draftees. Lots of cheap poontang. You may even want to re-up after reading this thriller."

Sandy Primm, author of
Short Time

PRAISE FOR REMF DIARY

"I, too, was a Saigon 'REMF.'... really brought home the tedium of REMF life.... what [the author] established is a ground of authenticity for the life of the REMF..."

> Timothy J. Lomperis, author of
> *Reading the Wind*

"I really enjoyed reading it. I especially liked the sub-plot of Madame Ky and how it connected with so many situations and aspects of American involvement in Vietnam."

> Susan Jeffords, author of
> "Born of Two Fathers:
> Gender and Misunderstanding in
> *Platoon*"

"[The] narrator is magnificently annoying, and I think [the author's] messages transcend him effectively. I was especially pleased with the way [he] ended the diary. Congratulations on writing a clever yet incisive book."

> Nancy Anisfield, author of
> *Vietnam Anthology, American
> War Literature*

"*REMF Diary* is a fascinating chronicle of one soldier's daily life in Vietnam, and a rare and untypical Veteran's memoir of Army service in that war."

> Alasdair Spark, author of
> "Flight Controls: The Social
> History of the Helicopter as a
> Symbol of Vietnam"

"*REMF Diary* is a long overdue account of a real 'truth' about the Vietnam War, that for most American participants it was a mixture of the exotic and the tedious, of glamour and boredom in duties spent behind the lines in routine tasks."

> Jeffrey Walsh, author of
> *American War Literature,
> 1914 to Vietnam*

"I liked it... it's accessible, moves along easily, and is as much concerned with telling a story as it is with technique... It is a highly credible character study of an interesting, if not always appealing, protagonist."

M.J. Naparsteck, author of
War Song and *A Hero's Welcome*

"*REMF Diary* is real and honest, funny and hard and sad in the way of bright comic moments and gentle gestures..."

Richard Curry, author of
Fatal Light and *The Wars of Heaven*

"I liked [the author's] courage,... courage to write a book like that. We need more rear-area books. If the bush was Dante's *Inferno*, then the rear was Sartre's *No Exit*."

William Crapser, author of
Remains: Stories of Vietnam

"*REMF* is a remarkable work.... [The] book is a camera and the style cinema verite. Blunt, unflinching, warts and all, [the author] captures a face of the Vietnam war that needs to be remembered."

Joe Rodriguez, author of
Oddsplayer

"... a good book in its depiction of the 'aspect' of war that is seldom portrayed, and, with regard to Vietnam, not done by anyone else."

Gordon Weaver, author of
"Under the World"

"I... devoured *REMF* in two sittings. I enjoyed it very much indeed.... [the author is] pretty well unique in addressing life at the Blunt End of War from the Enlisted Man's point of view."

Richard Holmes, author of
Acts of War

"At last, a Vietnam novel I can relate to.... I loved it. Willson's witty work brought back fond and not-so-fond memories of my former life as a pencil pusher with the illustrious 527th Personnel Company outside the city of Qui Nhon back in 1967-68.... This is a tour unlike any I'd read about in a Vietnam novel. And David Willson deserves the gratitude of all former REMF's for putting a stenographer (who, by the way, doesn't know how to take steno and refuses to do so) in the lead role in a Vietnam novel."

Marc Leepson
Veteran, October 1988

"... there is no combat, no broken bones, no gushing blood or flesh reduced to pulp. This story is not about grunts, guerrillas or Green Berets living on the knife-edge of daily murder and mayhem ... but rather the unsung and unrecognized vet who was fighting the paper war as well as the mama-san to get his laundry back.... Willson gives us an insight into the forgotten aspects of the war ... Nuance, subtlety and a wealth of authentic detail create an evocative sense of what it was like to be a REMF in Vietnam.... This novel about the boredom and banality of life in the war zone is more typical of Vietnam than are combat novels. Reality for most GIs was something far less romantic or dramatic than Larry Heinemann's *Close Quarters* or Gustav Hasford's *The Short Timers*, and far more like *REMF Diary* which says it simply and well."

Jean-Jacques Malo
The Fiction Review, September 1988

"Dear David,

"I liked your book a lot and it brought back vivid and deeply buried memories of that crazy AG office thing we all went through. Your tone is really confident, the descriptions and conversations have authority. The episodes are funny and affectionate. Even the broken diary rhythm works to communicate that day-after-day feeling, one foot in front of the next until it's over. It's an experience we share with inmates of jails and mental hospitals."

Robert Chatain, author of
The Ant War

THE REMF RETURNS

by David A. Willson

BLACK HERON PRESS
Post Office Box 95676
Seattle, Washington 98145

Published by:
Black Heron Press
Post Office Box 95676
Seattle, Washington 98145

ISBN 0-930773-21-7 (cloth bound)
ISBN 0-930773-22-5 (perfect bound)

TYPOGRAPHY BY DATAPROSE, SEATTLE
COVER DESIGN BY JEROME GOLD

THE REMF RETURNS

Preface

The U.S. Army snafued again. Yes, it's me, back. Not really. Not ever gone. No Japan. No home-going. It's as if nothing ever happened, Madame Ky-wise. Business as usual. Right back where I started.

THE REMF RETURNS

5 July 1967, Wednesday, 8:30 p.m.

I wish I could have parted from Saigon more sanguinely—or do I mean less sanguinely? I've done all the harm here I feel like doing, for now, anyhow.

I've soaked up the Saigon area as much as one can without living on the economy with a girl as did the narrator of *The Quiet American,* which I still think the best piece of writing on Vietnam that I've yet seen, fiction or so-called fact. I took some more pics today attempting to use up the film I've still got left to my old camera, but didn't quite.

Martin Luther King is on the radio right this minute, and his cultured voice and his precise enunciation make me yearn for Leadbelly, Cat-Iron or Blind Willie Johnson. When a blues poet speaking the Negro argot is accepted on radio as a spokesman for the Negro, then we'll have made progress.

King just said that he admires Clay for his courage in sticking to his stand on the draft, as an objector. I too think he is to be admired for this stand, as after all, he's putting money up where his mouth is (and a lot of money that'll take) and will lose much more than he gains by his decision.

Ding dong, the witch is dead, the radio sings.

Ed just played for me his cutting and commenting version that he's done on *A Day in the Life,* that Beatle thing. He would make a fine DJ of the satiric kind.

AFRTS just stammered off the air in the middle of a song so I'm now listening to a RVN station of French music, I think it is, but you know that foreign shit, it all sounds alike. One would think that English would be good enough for these damned people, it was good enough for OUR LORD to write the Bible in.

I just realized I'd not yet signed in, so I'll have to do that in a few minutes. STARK Terror at forgetting.

10:30 p.m.

I spent the rest of this eve packing some of my gear in preparation for THE BIG MOVE on Saturday. Later I'll have to start getting ready to load up all of our files and supplies and the rest of that stuff. I thought I was going to be spared the trauma of adjusting to Long Binh, but I was wrong. Wrong, like I've been about so many things in my life. I hate the thought of moving all that stuff, but it must be done.

I look forward to being out of the Army. All that freedom after more than a year of this restraint will be quite a jolt to my system, anomie will set in, and all sorts of Durkheimian syndromes will be in evidence. Really, I don't think it would be a terribly hard adjustment to make. From Long Binh to the States might be a different thing, however. I'll just have to wait and see. Maybe it will be a paradise up there the way everyone claims.

6 July 1967, Wednesday

It's 6:15 a.m. and I'm about to go to breakfast. I opened up the upstairs this morning, went to formation (I was one of the 6 men present in our platoon) and now will finish up this diary entry and off to break my fast in preparation for another unreasonable day. It's finished.

7:15 p.m.

Today most of the office moved to Long Binh. They spent yesterday loading up a big trailer, one that goes behind a semi, with desks, boxes, heavy unassembled file cabinets, etc. Because of events I wasn't involved so I avoided lifting anything very heavy. I'm not really very depressed but I've had a headache much of the day, which I'm just now shaking after a cooling shower and relaxing at the library reading some of the new stuff that came in today. A new Ed McBain novel, *8,000 Eyes,* and a poetry anthology called: *Where is Vietnam?, American Poets Respond,* ed. Walter Lowenfels, Doubleday Anchor original, $1.25 for a paperback, which is what they had. It's a very interesting book. One of the most interesting things about it is the large number of young poets that are included and the info in the back on them and the little magazines in which they've published.

I'm going to have to seriously start thinking of R&R and the money I'm going to need. $125 is the minimum for subsistence, $150 about as little as possible for a good time and more is needed if things will be purchased. I'd like to buy some things, of course, as I've not yet bought anything of real quality over here, but one should remember the poem by Robert Graves called "Neglectful Edward" in which he lists what he's brought his Nancy: "a rope of pearls and a gold earring, / And a bird of the East that will not sing. / A carven tooth, a box with a key—" and she replies: " 'God be praised you are back,' says she, / 'Have you nothing more for your Nancy?' " And of course I have learned from this lyric but didactic poem of Graves and I'll be no "Neglectful Edward", you can be certain. But will I have the opportunity to interact with my Darling after the incident at the dressmaker's? We'll see.

Only 4 months left, actually less. It's 107 days almost exactly, I think. That's not long, really. My lonesomeness is taking the form of a general malaise and deadheadedness, daydreaming, etc. Dead Head left earlier today for Long Binh, a truck piled high with his belongings, him sitting in the back with his bicycle and his M-14. Not that it's a dangerous trip, it's just the way the company wants the weapons transported.

I wonder if Long Binh's library will be like this one? They have very many of the new novels and every book that has been published on Vietnam, I'm convinced, mostly against the thing, of course. I wonder how the books are selected as there seems to be no bias other than maybe a slight liberal one.

No military censorship that I can detect either of periodicals or books. No far right mags or far left either. But plenty of stuff is printed in most of the mags against the Vietnam thing. And they have *M*, by John Sack, displayed on the counter in a special display of Vietnam-oriented books. That book shows the American forces in Vietnam to be frequently fouled up, stupid, etc.

I need to find money for R&R. I've been made a SP5, but that promotion has not solved my problems. I don't think I'd have made it if I'd gone in front of a board, but that's a problem I won't have to ever face.

About R&R. I plan to go to Hong Kong in late August or early September.

I was asked today by an officer if I'm thinking of making a career of the Army. He must be awful thick-headed if he doesn't realize my feelings on that subject. Just his asking the question makes me madder than hell, although I know it shouldn't. Goddamn him anyhow, that's just proof that he has no idea of my personality or beliefs. I'm a pacifist at best, and an anarchist at worst, and in any case I hate authority of any kind, and anyhow I've got many other plans. Maybe he was being ironical because he's aware of my little problems.

There is a dab of typing to do so I'll do it and write more this evening or later today anyhow.

9:00 p.m.

It's now 9:00 p.m. and I'm sitting waiting for 9:30 so I can shower and read in the sack 'til I fall asleep and I'm tired enough so that it won't take long. Most of the day was spent packing and moving with some typing and filing sprinkled here and there. Tomorrow will be a very big day, and then we'll leave Saturday morning. A truck will back down the drive into the office driveway and we'll load it up and *fini* Tan Son Nhut. I'll miss the privacy of a room with adjoining bath and refrigerator upstairs, I know. We may, four or five of us, chip in on a small refrigerator and then when we all leave in October sell it to someone else. We are going to need plenty of ice and cold drinks out at Long Binh for sure.

Tomorrow morning Charlie is going to pick up 12 detail men as I did this morning (a privilege we get for being SP5's) and we'll supervise them in the rest of the moving, especially the lifting and all other heavy work.

I've had almost all of my clothes cleaned and ironed and even have finagled a way to get a wall locker up there, so I hope things will be as nice as they can be anyhow, with no needless privation. Needed privation doesn't please me either. One thing is certain: It can't be as bad convenience-wise as is rumored.

I've been drinking Twink all day, and the unaccustomed sweetness of the drink had my stomach in knots for a while. I've noticed that over here drinking too much of a sweet drink will do that. I wonder if that is due to the heat? Or what? Tommy Roe is singing, "Oh Sweet Pea." It has a strange Dylanesque dissonance that a song like this wouldn't have had 5 years ago. "For Your Precious Love" by Oscar Tony, Jr. (I wonder what Senior

did?) just played and that somehow intensified my
nostalgia. The only things that are going to make
this last 3 months bearable are the SP5 and the
change to Long Binh that should make the time
pass faster, just because of the unfamiliarity. Also
the SP5 should keep me from the *worser* aspects of
the move. Stevie Wonder has a new one, "I Was
Born to Love Her", that is very Dylanesque. I'm
beginning to doubt my ears, and if I am I'd be the
first to. The Beatles are now singing "The Rain
Comes." A new song I've not heard before. Or an old
one I've not heard before. It would be on an album
if it were an old one though. Oh I don't know. I'm
so tired I'm going to go shower and I'll write more
later.

7 July 1967, morning

It's 5:50 and I'm on my way to formation almost.
"Young Love" by Sonny James is now playing. That
sold more than 3 million copies for him at the time
of its popularity, and continues to sell all the time.
It was the Tab Hunter version that I remember
from my youth. The song is more important to my
boyhood best friend John than to me. He's had an
experience that really hangs him up on the thing. I
can't remember who had the hit on that thing since
Hunter but there was at least one, wasn't there?
Time to leave. I hope I have time to type another
entry today before I pack up my machine for the
trek to LBJ Ranch (Long Binh Junction Ranch). As
I get paralysis of the hand trying to write.

9:15 p.m.

I'm sitting here in my denuded room bereft of a typewriter, listening to Sam the Sham and the Pharaohs sing "Oh That's Good, No That's Bad", a very fine song. We spent the day preparing for the move tomorrow. All the office equipment is boxed up and Charlie and I spent the evening packing up our own gear. We just moved it all out into the main office room and we have a prodigious quantity of stuff. I always collect junk, but I don't know where I'm going to put the shit at Long Binh. But tomorrow we'll find out. My hand is already paralyzed. I'm not a handwriter any more. This pen isn't the best either.

Those drivers who've been to LBJ already say that the only showers available are hot ones, and when the water is gone, it's gone. And one must wade 3 blocks through knee-deep red clay to get there. One gets 3 showers—one on the way up, one up there, and one on the way back—ha ha.

The billets supposedly leak profusely when it rains, which is all the time. One thing is nice — the area is secure, and there is no fear of infiltration and all that.

I'm all written out. My arm is gripped by pain and throbs in every knob. I'll write more in the morning.

8 July 1967, Saturday, 5:45 a.m.

I just finished up my packing while listening to the moldy oldies show. "The Eggplant that Ate Chicago" is on now. It's time for me to make the formation and then pick up my rifle, eat, and then leave, I guess, after loading everything on the truck.

Heard on AFRTS: A communications blanket that circles the world.

9:30 p.m., Saturday, Long Binh

It's a busy day I've just finished. Deadhead Ed, Charlie, John S. and I are set up in a new billet (barracks-type), 4 of us alone on the bottom floor, but it won't last. More people are bound to move in, but we have the best positions picked out. We've a full length wall mirror to put up to shave by in the morning. So far it's been a lot cooler up here, and it rains every few minutes.

The building we moved into isn't even half completed on the inside, but we put our desks in it anyhow and the room was also full of stepladders with gooks on them fixing the wiring in the ceiling. Oh yes, there's no ceiling or electricity either.

Tomorrow we all work to get things straightened out in the office. The typing is piled up to the nonexistent ceiling.

I had a cold shower tonight. I prefer them now. Besides, the hot water is boiling hot.

There are no company details yet, as the company is so fucked up. I hope they stay that way 'til I leave.

I hope to start typing entries tomorrow, as handwriting them is almost impossible. My hand gives up the ghost—as it has now—and my brain drags to a halt, too.

9 July 1967, Sunday, 6:50 a.m.

Good morning. I got up too late to eat breakfast this morning so it's going to be a hungry old day, 'til noon at least.

10:45 a.m.

It's a great feeling to be back behind a typewriter again, as the words flow out so much more naturally than with my poor crippled hand when holding a pen. I'll never be able to compose anything again without a machine to type on.

Our office is all set up, all we need is electricity and we'll be in fine shape. Kathy's typewriter doesn't work without the juice so that will be something I'll make sure is done as soon as it is possible. She will do the typing as much as possible.

The office arrangement is okay. I've got a good position in the room, except for the fact that Maj. Tief is looking directly across at me. I'm going to chow now, will finish when I return.

Later:

It's 12:45 and I'm back from lunch, which wasn't bad: fried chicken, potatoes-gravy, carrot sticks, huckleberry pie, 2 or 3 different things to drink, lots of ice, quite good chow for the Army. As good or better than the chow down at USARV Saigon. Col. Ebby was in the office while I was at lunch and announced a few small changes he wanted made in the room. I expressed surprise to the sergeant major that Col. Ebby had been here and he said yes, he'd been here most of the morning and where had I been to not see him. Doublethink again. Now if I were in the office from 7:15 a.m. until 11:00 a.m. and Col. Ebby arrived here at 11:15 and was here until he left for lunch at noon, that means that I was here more of the morning than Col. Ebby, right?

We have a refrigerator in our barracks, and have it full of Hamm's beer and soda. The Hamm's beer I scrounged up so it didn't cost a thing.

I guess I could be mopping the floor and washing the tops of the desks, but I really don't feel like doing that sort of thing. I'd rather lie down and read poetry while listening to Bo Diddly sing Pooten Tang on my little blue record player.

I'm going to have to find a laundry up here as I'm dirtying clothes just as always, if not faster.

When I say above that Maj. Tief is looking across at me I mean that his desk is looking across at me, as he's on R&R and is so potted I'm sure that he won't be able to see a thing. He was going to Taiwan where he has some friends who are very high in the old echelons, generals in fact, and he will have a very high time.

This headquarters in which our office is sits up
on a high hill surrounded by green vegetation and
countryside. All of this huge area was completely
denuded of vegetation, and the red laterite soil is
everywhere. A large quantity of it is here on the
floor. The dust blows everywhere except when it's
raining. Which is every couple of hours.

The dust blows especially vigorously when the
helicopters land and take off. Our office windows
overlook General Westmoreland's helicopter pad. I
pray that I get at least one ride on a helicopter
before I depart this country. I'm too smart to want
to be a helicopter door gunner (every other Army
clerk's wet dream.) All I want is one ride, but I
probably won't even get that. Life isn't fair.

I talked to Col. Rollins for a long time this
morning and his billets are no better than mine.
Twenty-five years in the Army and he has to put up
with completely unnecessary privation. It makes no
sense. This building is so unfinished it has no plug-
ins. A cord has been run down the middle of the
hall from which little extension cords run, providing
juice for those who are lucky. It's 1:10 right now,
and it's almost too dark for me to type without
squinting.

This evening I'm going to carry some of my
records back to my billets. I finally located all of my
personal boxes, as they were scattered all over hell
here in the various rooms which the office has. This
room we are in would be perfect if ol' Maj. Tief
were elsewhere. Like if he stayed in Okinawa. Or
Taiwan, or wherever he is.

Those damn NCOs keep poking their noses around. If I don't look busy they'll have me doing some dirty work nearby and I can't have that.

I just figured out why it was so dark. It's now raining very hard and the floors were wet before I could dash the 10 feet necessary to close the windows. Now it's stopped already. And I have to reopen the windows or suffocate. Re-open, I think.

Yes, I re-opened them and now a very strong wind is blowing through the room, a strong cool wind. The rain up here cools things off, which is different from Saigon.

The new office buildings here that aren't finished are of a huge US type of office building like those at the school at Fort Ben Harrison. When finished they will have central air conditioning, fluorescent lighting, latrines, shower rooms, all sorts of modern goodies. Telephones in every office. Now there is only one phone, and it's down the hall from us.

The club is okay. They haven't many chairs, but I'd rather drink at the billets. I have yet to find a barber shop but I don't worry about that. I do worry about libraries, but although there isn't one here, I have enough poetry to last me for a while. I borrowed (permanently) *The Oxford American Poetry Book,* which is a huge thing, and I also brought along the Untermeyer book, which is very large. These books give me enough poetry to get some idea of the poet at least to determine if I wish to read more of him. Louis Untermeyer seems to always pick the dullest poetry of the poets he includes, and further he leaves out some of the finer poets. The *Oxford* is a little better, but it goes up 'til only 1950 and it's the poetry since that I'm most interested in:

Roethke's later poems, James Dickey and that other poet whose name I always forget.

Col. Ebby just came in and is followed by Lt.Col. Rollins. He says that his billets are much worse than mine and I believe him. Both he and Lt.Col. Rollins think the whole move is ridiculous, but neither of them can do a thing about it. Lt.Col. Rollins is getting so short that he doesn't care, but Col. Ebby is a little short-tempered, rather, a lot short - tempered, about the inconvenience of the move. They also figure that it will cost us about 5 million dollars more to move before the buildings are complete. This is really the world of Catch 22. It's more apparent now and during this kind of absurd nonsense than at other more normal times.

2:30 p.m.

We just moved the room furniture around and it looks better than it did, although I still am across from Maj. Tief, which seems to be an irremediable problem. I hope to find a remedy for it before he returns from his 7-day vacation, but I doubt if I will.

It just started to rain again and both colonels got their own windows. They are still (even Lt.Col. Rollins) two of the best men in the section to work with. The only other officer I work with is the administrative officer, Maj. Richards, and we get along fine so my last 3 months here should be painless and without conflict within the office. The company also seems as though it will be a mini-mum interference and that's the way I hope it will stay.

Lt. Col. Rollins is turning out the work which I hope I'm not expected to do today. I'm a lazy bones.

This evening we will put my wall locker together which will be a character builder, but not my idea of a pleasant evening.

The wind blows through this room so fiercely that Lt. Col. Rollins not only can't light a cigarette, but he can't keep it lit long enough to take a drag off the thing once he lights it.

I guess I'm beginning to repeat myself so I'll end this entry for now.

Later:

It's 9:30 and I've been trying to get my area straightened away since 6:00. I've got a wall locker built and all my stuff arranged therein. My foot locker too is arranged, the mirror, full length, is mounted on the wall. Now if there were water, all would be right with this microcosm. No water on Sundays as the gook is off.

Lex Barker is one of my favorites, along with Victor Mature and Cornell Wilde, two other very underrated actors who have much talent. Barker had an interesting part in "La Dolce Vita."

Stephen Foster played by Mantovani is on right now—hybrid hybrids—mutated mutants. My record player doesn't work here as the cycles changed from 50 to 60—or was it 60 to 50? Anyhow, it doesn't work. Sorry about that.

10 July 1967, Monday, 6:15 a.m.

Morning, and I'm all ready to go break my fast.
I've shined my boots and brass, made my bed,
shaved and all that other bull shit. I'm ready for a
new day. I hope Kathy's at work today as I don't
feel like doing anything except filing and logging.

4:00 p.m.

We've got lights in here now and things are
shaping up. So far the weather here has been quite
cool, especially at night, which I think nice. Of
course it rains often, but the Army raincoat sheds
that with no difficulty. I look forward to a shower
tonight as I feel dirty going without one even for
one day.

Tonight we continue to try and get our billet in
living condition. We'll move our TV in and set up a
shelf for it. This morning I shaved at the full-length
mirror from a basin of water set out the night
before on a field table, and it was about as close
and convenient as one can have it without running
water. I could have hot water for shaving if it
meant much to me just by putting on a pot of water
to heat on the hot plate when I first get up, but I'm
sure I'll not do that ever. I'm much too lazy.

The work day here will be from 7:30 'til 5:00,
which is a nice short day if it lasts.

Today at noon Charlie and I went to the laundry. One small Vietnamese laundry takes care of
the entire billet area, so we had to wait in line for
more than 30 minutes. A waste of valuable leisure
time, I think. I would rather read poetry or mysteries or anything. The lights just went off and I

was handed a big bunch of crap to do over. I'd just finished it a few minutes prior to the beginning of this entry. I'll go now and write more later.

7:30 p.m.

I'm back at the hooch, showered, relaxed and pissed off at the undecided work schedule. "Did You Ever Have to Make Up Your Mind?" just played.

Ed is right now describing the night he dragged into every bar in town, walked up to comely bar girls and said "Okay?" with a question mark. He got a few weird responses.

Peaches and Herb's "For Your Love" is now playing. They are too much, as they say. I do like them.

Ed (Dead Head) just put up my mosquito net for me—there are a few of the things here. It's not really buggy though.

I'm going to read for a while, nothing more to write now. It's 9:30.

11 July 1967, Tuesday, 5:50 a.m.

Time for me to dodder off to breakfast and then to work. That malaria pill is working on my system, as always. I'll be glad to be able to quit taking those damn orange things.

12:00 noon

It's high noon and I'm waiting for Kathy to get
back from lunch so that I'll be able to go. I'm very
hungry and the chow hall closes at 1:00. Between
12:30 and 1:00 there is nothing much left over to
eat, just scraps and nothing to drink except that
reconstituted milk. I'm sure that is a temporary
situation, however. If it continues this way I'll be
forced to take an early lunch myself. The schedule
here is still fucked up and it displeases me mightily. Kathy must leave by 5:00 as WAC dinner is
served between the hours of 5:00 and 6:00 and she'll
not return. One of us must be on duty at all times
during the day in our room. Therefore if she leaves
every day at 5:00 and the work day lasts 'til 7:30 as
is planned for the future, I'll never again eat
dinner. That doesn't seem to me to be a viable plan
so I shall work something else out, I'm sure. Also
that means WACs never will have to burn trash.
They are a bit more equal than the rest of us, like
the pigs in *Animal Farm*. I'm not a stolid Louis
L'Amourean hero, but a whiner. I think whiners get
further. In the long run. My run hasn't been long
enough yet for me to know.

Obviously I won't work every night 'til 7:30.
That's the kind of thing soldiers go to my office
about, and I'd do the same.

Today the work is piled up to the ceiling as all
of the correspondence that's been trailing behind us
has finally gotten here. I don't care though, as I'm
giving it all to Kathy to type. I figure her day is so
short that she can do a little more while she's here
to compensate. (She gets here at almost 8:00 a.m.
while everyone else must be here at 7:30 a.m. I got

here at 6:30 this morning in an attempt to write in this diary, but actually ended up working most of the time.)

Charlie was kept here so late last night that he missed a meal. That's a huge sin in my estimation. Next time they keep him late we'll all stay (6 clerks) and wait for him as a subtle protest against the unfairness of his being kept late.

Later:

It's 6:15. Charlie burned the trash from 5:00 'til 6:00 so nobody got mail. Also the WACs went home at 5:00 so I'm here until closing, whatever that will be. When I get back to the barracks I want to curl up with a book or read some poetry.

Tomorrow there will have to be a conference with the sergeant major and the clerks to attempt to arrive at some fair method of distributing all of the extra details. There must be a solution.

And Later:

It's 7:15. Now to go back to the barracks and relax.

Later yet, 10:00 p.m.

I'm showered and all clean—for naught. I got back here to the area and ate dinner at 7:30—ham sandwich, vanilla ice cream, beets, ice tea—good old re-up chow. The area is noisy as hell, so I'm going to cut this short and finish in the morning.

12 July 1967, Wednesday, 5:30 a.m.

I'm up and ready to go to breakfast. I'm going to eat and go to the office and hide in my room and try to read some more of Agatha Christie's novel *Cards on the Table,* a Hercule Poirot mystery. I hope the sergeant major and clerk conference holds no unpleasant revelations in store.

"... the new generation of brave men struggling to win peace in this embattled land."
    —*Stars & Stripes, 10 July 1967*

10:00 a.m.

Lt. Col. Rollins just told me with admiration that he's made less progress with me than with any other clerk he's had in 20 years. I consider that a compliment, and I think he meant it as one. He was just pointing out what I already know. I have an innate inability to adjust to other people's methods of doing things. Sometimes that's a good trait, sometimes a bad one.

Charlie and I have almost certainly decided to go on R&R together to Singapore in September unless the office balks at the idea, and they'd best not as that would displease us mightily.

Lt. Col. Rollins just had a discussion with me of obscene statuary. He has some Nepalese sculpture that depicts a woman astraddle a man, also a set of monkeys, hear no evil etc., one of which has his hands over his balls. Rollins isn't a bad fellow. He's been reading *Tin Drum* ever since he arrived in country and is only on page 400 odd.

I just got an endorsement to type. The electricity is off so Wacky Kathy is off cavorting with one of her little friends.

Later:

It's 12:05 and I'm waiting for Kathy to come back from lunch so I'll be able to go. I must be in a good mood, because I just read *The Stars and Stripes* and almost everything in it amused me. Articles like "Porkers Get a Snootful," "Baby Whooping Crane Dies; Mom Sits on Him," "Miss Wales' Tights Almost Squeezed Her Out of Contest," "Vivien Leigh Dies; Suffered From TB," "Denver Hit by Floods," etc. I guess I must be in a good mood. It just started raining furiously. And I'll soon be out in the stuff.

The word just came out on promotion this month. Our company is allotted 3 slots versus unlimited last month, and it is said those eligible for promotion will have to go in front of a board. Charlie and I lucked out. We were put in the only month since I've been here that we could have had such luck.

It's now 12:15 and old Kathy is not yet back. She's a loser.

The Vietnamese workmen who were putting in our ceiling were eating their little meals of rice and vegetables next door a few minutes ago. They then finished their meals and sat and jabbered at each other in rapid Vietnamese. During this stage of their lunch hour Lt. Col. Rollins sat at his desk wooden-faced waiting for the next stage of their lunch hour: sleepy time. This is where they are now. They stay in this stage longest. I'm going to check distribution and will write more later.

6:07 p.m.

It's getting later and later and finally a policy has been established for working until 6:30. I just had a discussion with Col. Ebby about the WACs' working hours and the unfairness of the policy of working until 6:30 every night and getting the tag and scrag end of chow. I'm bitter, bitter and whiny when I feel that I'm getting less than the best of the deal. I'm going to close up shop now and take off. I'll finish this entry at the hooch. Soon we have our sergeant major/clerk conference.

Later:

Nothing much resolved at the sergeant major/-clerk conference. Same old shit. Everything will come out in the wash. This is just the shakedown cruise, etc. I think the sergeant major served three years in the Navy in his misspent and misbegotten youth.

One (the only) piece of potentially earth-shattering news — the sergeant major is leaving. He's gotten some plum post somewhere (mum's the word) and he'll be replaced soon by a new sergeant major, a Sergeant Major Smith. That name made my stomach lurch. It can't be my old nemesis from Italy, Master Sergeant Smith. There must be dozens, even hundreds of Sergeant Smiths in the U.S. Army. I'm just being my paranoid self. Italy and my

debacle there (his, really) are finally forgotten—
actually eclipsed by my recent escapades. Escapades,
by the way, about which everyone seems to have
developed amnesia. I'm sure I'm just thinking the
worst. Time will tell. I'll discuss it all with Col.
Ebby.

13 July 1967, Thursday, 5:30 a.m.

I went to bed last night very early—after my
discussion of working hours with Col. Ebby. He
stormed down to the administration office. We'll
know today what effect he had.

I'm listening to country-western music. Flatt and
Scruggs just sang "It's Only the Wind, Ma" and it
was followed by Justin Tubbs' "The Second Thing
I'm Going to Do When I Get Home is Put My
Suitcase Down." I'm off to breakfast now.

10:30 a.m.

Here I am sitting in my desk with nothing to do
'til the next draft hits the colonel's out box. Today I
learned that part of our office (Col. Ebby's division)
will be moving into an adjoining room. Col. Ebby
asked me who I thought should move in there and I
opted for Kathy and Major Tief, as a ploy to get
them both out of my hair at the same time. That is
what will be done. The room is finished and is now
being cleaned so the stuff will be moved in later
today.

Major Tief is not back from his Taiwan R&R yet.
I'm glad. He said he'd get me a Taiwan love book
illustrated with a selection of arcane sexual posi-

tions. That would be nice as I'm sure he's the fellow who would have the contacts to procure an item of that nature; that is, if he leaves his bed long enough to take care of any business of that nature.

Today Kathy spent most of her time down the hall typing, as she gets a thrill being close to the new clerk. Her beau, Joe, just returned from a 10-day inspection trip and he's not getting the attention he was wont to have. As the bard says: La Donna mobile! Right? Well, some of them are.

One thing about Col. Rollins, he's not in any rush to get the work done. He lets it sit in his basket for days. Lt.Col. Prince would go through it like a whirlwind, keeping three clerks busy typing for one day and then we'd sit for a couple of days with nothing. Lt.Col. Rollins just dribbles out the work so it's the same all the time. Slow. That's fine with me. I must soon get a haircut and pick up my laundry and also bring my fan to the office. So much to do. All of it of no importance or relevance to real life whatever.

It would be nice to have Saturday afternoon and Sunday off but apparently we work a 7-day-per-week schedule up here. I hope I'm wrong. I've got some stuff to do so will write on this later.

7:30 p.m.

I'm just getting finished here. I'm going to shower and go right to bed. It's been a long hard day.

14 July 1967, Friday, 7:45 a.m.

Today we got the word on company details—E-5s and down, that includes me. This week I'm on Monday and Saturday—all of both days. The news made Col. Ebby unhappy, but there's naught to be done. With me working only four days next week Col. Ebby and Col. Rollins will have fun. Old Kathy now refuses to do anything. They've been trying to get rid of her but I doubt they'll be successful.

Kathy is from Vermont. Why is she in the Army? Because she's fucked up. I can't think of any other reason. Bad home environment or something, I suppose. She'd say that she wanted to travel and see excitement. She's too fat and dumb to be a stewardess.

Bob Dylan is now singing "Everybody must get stoned" and it brings old Indy back—back—only three months, one week 'til I'm gone from here.

Col. Ebby gave me a ride to chow tonight, which is a courtesy that I appreciated. The weekend schedule is minimal to allow us to get haircuts, rest, etc.

Now "When a Man Loves a Woman" is playing— Percy Sledge. That brings tears to my eyes.

The schedule for me is off Saturday afternoon, all day Sunday, detail in company on Monday—back at work on Tuesday.

I've not yet made it through the Agatha Christie I'm reading. I don't seem to get enough leisure. I should have leisure this weekend. With scheduled detail now the company has no excuse to shanghai me out of the sack to dig mud.

Believe it or not, Deadhead Ed was giving haircuts tonight. What a fellow to give haircuts.

The haircuts he gave are very uneven and disreputable looking.

Tomorrow I really plan to get a haircut. I think I'll get it cut short—less trouble—and it'll grow out, at least it always has. Now I plan to read some poetry—William Carlos Williams, Emily Dickinson, while listening to more music and then to sleep.

15 July 1967, Saturday, 5:45 a.m.

I'm listening to a take-off recording of The Rock Island Line—that makes fun of the pig-iron part of the song. ABC double XYZ cats in the cupboard, etc. I'm now off to breakfast.

> *Don't number your fish after your*
> *rooster dong dies*
> *   —Folk Saying*

7:10 p.m.

I'm in the sack relaxing, listening to Pete Seeger sing from the Columbia Bad Men album. It's the folk music hour on AFRTS. This brings back old times.

Today in the *Stars and Stripes* an obit lists LCPL (Marine) David M. Bradley, Pullman, Washington. Could that be the one I know? I hope not, as he was a good fellow. It would be like him to be a Marine.

I got my laundry back this afternoon and also got a haircut. I then went back to the office (fool that I am) to get my mail, and I got roped into spending the rest of the afternoon in the office.

We had a flap there with that scheming Kathy. She told her commanding officer that everybody picked on her, that I made her do all the work, etc.

She cried, sobbed her little heart out. She's the original conniving woman.

The result was that all of us were admonished to not kid or tease her about her motley inadequacies, just treat her matter-of-factly. Lt. Col. Rollins and Col. Ebby are both teases as am I. It will be hard. She's a hateful creature. She'll be handling the job by herself two whole days next week and I don't expect her to do too well.

I'm itchy all over so guess I'll go shower and finish this later.

8:10 p.m.

I've not showered yet. I listened to them play the rest of Bad Men—"Cryderville Jail"—and Old Harry sing those cowboy songs. Now Roy Acuff is on Grand Ole Opry singing "Wabash Cannonball."

I've almost finished the Agatha Christie novel, which I'll now finish.

Bill Monroe is now singing "Out the Cold Cold World." Great stuff.

Grampa Jones is now singing "Roll On Buddy Roll On." Shades of Uncle Dave Macon.

Now the Fruit Jar Drinkers are singing and pickin'. Their personnel includes Barry Macon (Dave's son) and Sam and Kirk McGhee. Smith wasn't there for some reason. Maybe death.

"I was born in East Virginia. I don't want your greenback dollar." Finer folk music on Grand Ole Opry than on the folk music show. At least more of it.

Mother Maybelle Carter is on now. Such good music.

A little spider dropped down on me a few minutes ago and the little hairs on me itch like a million little crawly spiders. Not a comfortable feeling. I guess I'll have to shower sometime soon.

Maybelle is now playing her autoharp. Sounds better than Alice Stuart, but she's not singing. Reminds me of that sad old country "ballit", "Buy 14 Beers for Myself."

9:20 p.m.

I'm back from the shower refreshed, wearing doggy-smelling T-shirt and shorts from the local laundry, listening to Fascination Waltz—which of course reminds me of "Love in the Afternoon," that Audrey Hepburn/Gary Cooper movie, one of my favorites. A great steam bath episode in it. Now to read some poetry, Delmore Schwartz perhaps, then to sleep.

16 July 1967, Sunday, 5:15 p.m.

I got up at about 9:00 this morning, really I just woke up and read some poetry for a while, shaved, breakfasted (really an early lunch), and then went around to a couple of PXs in the area with Charlie. At about 11:00 we were in the office for what little mail was here. Tomorrow I'm on detail in the company all day.

Ed and Joe left on R&R yesterday for Hawaii without signing out, so they are on a 7-day AWOL. That's very typical of both of them as they are irresponsible.

How safe is it up here, I wonder? The WACs are

here, that should answer that. Very, very safe, safer than Saigon as anything could be. That's what's so dull about it. No place to go that isn't Army.

Time to go eat and I'll finish this later this eve.

Later:

It's 8:10, I'm watching Dick Van Dyke, one I've not seen. Dick just pounded on a desk, disrupting the picture. Dick is buying a nutria coat wholesale through one of Buddy's shady friend's friends. Dick is trying it on. It's a wacky wiggy show. There are implications of drag.

It's over now. The picture on the TV set here is very good, an indication that it was the Saigon current. "Get Smart" is now on.

Oh yes, I'm watching TV from the sack. A good place to be, but I'm very thirsty and the club's a block away. "Bonanza" is on now.

17 July 1967, Monday Morning

It's 6:35, we have had our first formation, and while we were stumbling around trying to find our places the band came marching out of the shadows John Philip Sousa-ing a march. We had to run and break formation to avoid being marched into the cold, cold ground. Time to exchange sheets!

6:45 p.m.

Today was an interesting and profitable day. I traded my size 11 double narrow jungle boots

(newly acquired) for a pair of 10R jungle boots, my
size. I got two new packaged sheets and a new
packaged wool blanket, all of which are on my bed
and I'm on my bed, freshly scrubbed and wiser from
a day spent in a loosely supervisory status over
shit-burning detail. A very interesting procedure
(and educational), and also a police detail, some
sawing, and miscellaneous other stuff.

Also today I saw Carter from Steno 21—blond,
blue-eyed southern guy. He made SP5 on 28 June.
After the day was over (4:45) I went to the office.
Also I had time to drop off my laundry at Jose's. It
was a leisurely, unhurried day, and it didn't rain
one all day 'til 4:40. And it's still raining.

While we were working today one of the drum-
mers was practicing in a shower stall, a little
portable building with tremendous acoustic qual-
ities. Sounded like a thousand Krupas gone mad—
and all we could see of him was his cap on the
ledge and occasionally his head popping over the sill
after a particularly vicious barrage.

All the guys just came in from the office all
agog with news. General Palmer put out a bulletin
—no more book reading or letter writing, just
jungle fatigues at the office—one must be working
all day. Also the WACs pulled more shenanigans—
those sweethearts. We're also now divided into
teams again. They also tell me that the old sergeant
major is gone (overnight) and a new one is firmly in
place. A Sergeant Major Smith, one who truly loves
enforcing Gen. Palmer's new order, one with a
spectacular handlebar moustache and, scuttlebutt
further has it, one who served a tour of duty in
Italy not so very long ago. My Master Sergeant
Smith, now newly minted sergeant major. My neme-

sis from Italy has reared his ugly head. It's a small fucking world. My Army world would make a broom closet seem as spacious as the Gobi Desert.

One day I'm gone from work and the heavens fall in. Ah well, I will adjust. I always do. I'm a kind of chameleon, I guess. Also I'm sneaky.

The Four Tops are now singing "The Same Old Song"—ain't that the truth!

"Monday Morning" by the Mamas and the Papas is on and Indy comes flooding back.

The Coasters—"Yakety Yak" is on now. Fine rockin' spirit.

On 22 July I'll get three more pair of jungle fatigues. Big deal. But I'll need them. I'll have to look really strak now.

What do I see when I turn out the lights? The face of my clock. Whenever I'm awakened by the cold or the artillery all I see is the clock face—2:30 it said. My head whirls with thoughts.

The Army does take care of its own, of which I'm one for three more months. Then *fini*. Aretha Franklin's now singing "R-E-S-P-E-C-T."

"Combat" just came on TV, but the picture is too bad for me to enjoy watching it. I've got a runny nose, slight sore throat, etc., from the chill nights here—and the rainy cool days—and the sneezes.

There are movies at Long Binh, but I've not the time nor the inclination. I'm too short to so spend my time.

Oh yes, it's rumored that the Nha Trang field office will move in with us. That means Dave C. will be back—up here actually—a general is after him for a steno—SHIT!!!

9:10 p.m.

Time for me to go take a piss, and then read awhile in my *Blues Unlimited* before sleep. I'll write a note in the morning.

18 July 1967, Tuesday Morning

It's 5:55. Charlie and I just ate breakfast and now we're off to work right after formation.

9:05 p.m.

The Smothers Brothers show just came on, and they are doing their monologue. Nancy Sinatra is on. She's not my favorite. "These boots . . ."

Well, on the surface of it, everything was peaches and cream between me and Sergeant Major Smith. He's my Sergeant Smith alright, handlebar moustache and all. My nemesis from Italy. The man who left me carrying the can, the man who ruptured the delicate fabric of my U.S. Army career and catapulted me into the war zone here in Vietnam, where every day I've been in jeopardy as an ignorant slow-moving target.

He was smooth as silk as always. "No hard feelings. Water under the bridge. Just do a good job and nothing to fear." The usual facile bullshit. He shook my hand and said yards of all the right conciliatory things. Typical of him. Butter wouldn't melt in his mouth.

I had to keep reminding myself that this is the guy who was selling U.S. Army equipment (arms) to German nationalists in South Tyrol, and when clerical work of mine inadvertently threatened to expose him, he framed me (or tried to) as being implicated in the South Tyrol People's Party's unsuccessful assassination attempt on Italian Premier Aldo Moro. I barely escaped hanging for that one. It did appear that I was involved, but once again it was my innocent affection for an olive-skinned peasant girl which had resulted in my being in the wrong place at the wrong time.

The good Master Sergeant Smith got promoted. I got busted to Private E-1 and posted to Vietnam. I owe him one and will do everything I can to see that it comes to pass. I will seize the opportunity.

Bygones be bygones—no fucking way, Jose.

After my encounter with the sergeant major today it took me most of the day to straighten out my logging and filing systems from Kathy's having had solo control on Monday when I burned shit. She did all the typing today and will from now on if I can get away with it.

I'm now going to read *My Secret Life* and eat some peanut butter cookies Charlie's mom sent.

19 July 1967, Wednesday Morning

It's 6:10. Just ate breakfast, had formation, and here I am ready to go to the office to do battle. I read *My Secret Life* last night until 11:00 and then didn't sleep much during the night due to the noise and my cold, which isn't really improving.

9:30 p.m.

No shower water tonight, and there'll be plenty of bitching tomorrow. My toes itch. As I've been reading *My Secret Life* that's not all that itches. It's an enjoyable book but I think Casanova's more interesting because he describes not only his secret life but his public life as a con-man, politician, etc. The exuberance of the narrator of this book is commendable, also his lack of perversions such as whipping, beating, pain, refusal of favors, etc.

Today was a usual busy day at work, busier than usual due to Major Tief's eternal fussing. That man tempts me to head-knocking, but with Sergeant Major Smith prowling around, Major Tief and his fussing fade to oblivion. I wonder when Smith will show his hand?

I still have my cold. A dandy it is, too.

Kathy is still going with Joe, is still engaged to a sap in the States who she writes to, and goes out on Joe whenever she gets a chance, all without qualms of conscience I'm sure.

I'm going down to the shower. Back in a while.

Later:

It's 10:20 and I had a lukewarm shower. The truck driver must have left his truck in the sun all afternoon while he got a piece behind the wood pile.

Today I spent an hour of my lunch hour-and-a-half cleaning my rifle. What a waste of time.

Time for bed. I'll write an entry in the morning.

20 July 1967, Thursday Morning

I'm on my way to work. A little behind the old

schedule.

9:00 p.m.

Today was a piss-poor day. I'm showered and in a good mood right now, but the day itself was shitty. Kathy got the afternoon off, leaving me a huge quantity of work, most of which I screwed up. I suspect Sergeant Major Smith's hand in this development. He always had a weakness for WAC clerk-typists and he knows her absence will have an impact on my life. She needs *no* encouragement to be gone. Kathy *will* do it over tomorrow. I have detail all day Saturday, and don't know yet if I'll work Sunday. Major Tief is on duty Sunday. If the two of us were stuck in the same room all day, I'd not be able to maintain a civil tongue. Ah well, everything always works out, they say, and we know just how it works out. Not for the better.

Right now "The Fugitive" is on. The police are depicted as stupid and brutal as usual. I'm almost tempted to try being a cop for a while when I get out of the Army just to find out from the inside what it's like. Probably it's very different from the stereotype.

Today Charlie got a letter from his grandmother, enclosing a clipping about Hong Kong—rioting, curfew, etc. That's a grandma for you, always precautioning. I don't think Charlie and I will go there, but it's not been ruled out, depending on the political situation. If Red China has taken over I don't think I'd like to go there, although it would be interesting.

I'm going to bed now. I'll write an entry in the

morning.

21 July 1967, Friday Morning

It's 5:55. I just ate eggs, oranges, toast and jam for breakfast. Now—the big formation.

8:15 p.m.

I'm on my bunk, just showered, listening to James and Bobby Purify sing "Bend Over, Let Me See Your Tailfeathers" and watching "Gunsmoke."

Nina Simone is singing, and now I know where Dave Van Ronk got his singing style.

Today was a fairly okay day, but I'm rather bad tempered these days because of the hammer of Sergeant Major Smith hanging over my head. I need a focus for my life.

I work on Sunday. I learned today also I spend all day tomorrow on shit detail. Is that a coincidence? I doubt it. I hope I can spend some time Sunday reading. That would be nice.

Right now three of the four male clerks on my team are on R&R so when trash needs burning I do it, alone. It's not really hard but it's one more thing that pisses me off. With Sergeant Major Smith here I see meaning in everything, every shadow is a monster.

I believe my cold is going away. It will be nice to not be hawking greenies all day. That at least would be something positive.

A funny story is going around about General Cole. The latrines for the command building in which I work are all lined up in a row by rank

(Generals' latrine, several Officers' latrines, and Enlisted Men's latrines). Earlier this week a fork lift operator was moving these outdoor latrines around—so they'd be better situated.

The fellow drove his machine up to the General's latrine, banged it several times with his lift, got his fork under it, and lifted it three or four feet off the ground. Then he heard a screeching noise from the latrine and dropped it with a jolt to the ground. With his dignity badly battered, General Cole made a swift exit. It's a story, not a joke, but it's Army for sure.

The radio just wished everybody a swinging weekend. Yeah, only two more working days 'til Monday.

I'm going to read for a while and write more later.

Later:

It's 10:00. There's an office party one week from this Sunday at a boat dock near Saigon—steak, booze, a band, water skiing—the whole bit. Maybe the sergeant major will get drunk and drown while water skiing. There's a thought.

Johnny Carson is on now—and it's thundering terrifically outside.

22 July 1967, Saturday, 7:40 p.m.

Today was detail day. I hammered, burned shit, dug holes, and all the rest of the shtick, and thought malign thoughts of Sergeant Major Smith.

I'm listening to the folk music program. He's

playing people like Nancy Ames singing Woody
Guthrie, which is disappointing, as you'd guess.

The sergeant let us off detail at 4:00, at which
time I got a haircut in a barber shop that has
moved in across the street.

The Terriers, the Chad Mitchells—real folk—
now just were played.

Now Logan English, that old friend of Woody
Guthrie, is singing a talkin' blues. I remember
when I saw him at the Bunkhouse in Vancouver.
Now Pat Boone is singing "Ave Maria"—a folk
song? Come on!

There's a guy bugging me right now. Our barracks is the place all the transients stay overnight.
I'd just as soon not talk to him, so I don't, but it's
hard to write an entry over his jabbering. I think
I'll try reading a book to drive him away. Will write
more later.

23 July 1967, Sunday Morning

I never did get shut of that fellow. It's now 6:00
and I'm on my way to chow and the office.

8:30 p.m.

Today wasn't too bad. This morning Major Tief
was in the office so I went for water and stayed
until almost mail time. Went for mail, came back,
went to lunch and Tief was gone and I saw him no
more. Hardly saw Sergeant Major Smith either.

Ed and Joe came back from R&R today. Ed
brought me a can of Brasso for my brass, I opened
it, poured it on a cloth, sat the open can on the

floor and promptly tripped on it, spilling most of it.
Brasso is impossible to get over here. I'm such a
clumsy fellow. It's true.

I spent most of the day writing a love poem for
My Darling. It's in the lyric category. I've been
reading K. Patchen's love poems and am a bit
influenced and greatly moved by them. They are
very differently arranged and put together.

The only other poet to approach his impact in
love poems is e.e. cummings. They write poems of
love that cause me to feel their pain.

"Get Smart" is on and I think I'll watch it a
while.

...."Get Smart" is now off. I'm going to sleep
now.

24 July 1967, Monday, 5:55 a.m.

Formation is just a gasp or two away. I just had
breakfast. Last night I read *The Crying of Lot 49*
for a while. That's a funny psychedelic type of book.
I'd think it'd be popular.

Time to go out and stand tall.

1:00 p.m.

This morning the Army band marched at us
again out of the darkness under the water tower
where they hide and we ran for the ditches on
either side of the road to avoid being trampled.
They wait until everyone is all formed up in even
ranks before they begin the thing. It's rather
entertaining, in a Pynchonesque way.

5:45 p.m.

This afternoon Major Tief asked for the car to run some errands so I pissed him off by asking Col. Ebby if I could go along and stop at the PX for stuff I needed. Of course he said he would let me, so I went along and got to see Major Tief in action at the salvage yard trying to "procure" a jeep for his use in a nonofficial manner. We bumped into Sergeant Major Smith at the yard. Butter wouldn't melt in his mouth. He's up to something. I guess Tief will get a jeep eventually. And probably Sergeant Major Smith will get his, too.

I'm going to try to save my money for the next weeks 'til Charlie and I go on R&R to Hong Kong or wherever we're going from 4 September to 10 September, approximately. I'd like to get a pair of snakeskin boots for myself, but they'd be rather ostentatious for any but hippy-type wear. With a beard they'd be appropriate.

I'll write more later as I've got some little things to do the last few minutes in the office.

25 July 1967, Tuesday Morning

It's 6:00 and I went to bed last night at 8:00, almost immediately after I arrived at the barracks. I feel very rested, so much so that I woke up several times last night thinking it was 5:00. Now it's 6:05, I went to formation. Now I'm about to go to work. I'm listening to the news of the negro revolution in the States, Detroit in particular.

11:45 a.m.

Lt. Col. Rollins is gone today, getting his retirement physical, Col. Ebby and Kathy are lunching (separately), and God knows where Major Tief is, as he could be anywhere and probably is.

How's old Long Binh been treating me? Not badly and not goodly. I'm due for a day off this Sunday, but I'm pessimistically awaiting assignment to a company detail on that day. And I'm sure Sergeant Major Smith would cooperate fully if not actively conniving to give me the assignment. If I get one I'll quietly do it, and then the next day file a complaint on a 1559 with Col. Ebby about inequities in the system, etc.

Kathy just returned from lunch as I was wrapping up a diatribe against the company details and the possibility of my getting one on Sunday and being prevented from attending the party. Most of it was a crescendo of "fucks" and the like, so she came through the door with a red face and a giggle. Big deal.

Dead Head Ed is doing fine. He didn't get an Article 15 for missing the obligation of signing out so that he was AWOL for 7 days while on R&R. Lucky Ed. I don't see much of him these days as he works four or five rooms away from me and we are on different duty teams.

Later:

It's now 7:17 and I just burned trash. On 15 August the Nha Trang Field Office in which Dave C. is a Steno will be moving in with this headquarters, so they'll be right here with us and we'll have one more clerk, Traywick, to burn trash, etc., and countless NCO's to hang like millstones around our necks. One senior NCO albatross is enough.

A few minutes ago I was slamming on my filing cabinet with an "out" box trying to get the jammed lock closed, a ritual I go through every night, but tonight for the first time Col. Ebby was in the office and the noise (akin to the sound of a locomotive hitting another locomotive head-on) bothered him a little. He came over to show me the scientific way to close it, failed miserably as I knew he would, and retired to his corner of the room. Now I will wait 'til he leaves the room and with truly fearsome noise and force will slam the thing shut. I just hope it will unlock in the morning. That would be a pretty kettle of fish if it didn't, as the bard says.

Tonight I hope to get deep into *The Crying of Lot 49,* which I have read about 42 pages of and enjoy much. I feel very grimy and dirty: coffee grounds stuck to my Adam's apple, carbon black on my ears, orange peel residue stuck under my nails along with cigarette ashes and other detritus of the great midden into which I delve every other day, it seems.

Today an SOP on company activities came through the office, and buried amongst the verbiage Charlie and I triumphantly found a clause relating the the use of SP5s, E-5s, and Sergeant E-5s. They shall be CQs in the company. E-4s and below will pull details, CQ orderly, head count. That includes us out. Charlie double buck-slipped the thing (an impressive procedure) to Sergeant Major Smith, and it will travel across the desks of the powers that could be if they wanted, tomorrow. It will be seen what results, if anything except lost tempers and retribution.

I guess I'll toddle off to my quarters now and shower and sack out.

10:00 p.m.

I just watched the Smothers Brothers, with Johnny Winters, Nancy Wilson, Jefferson Airplane —a good show, Winters especially.

A while ago I had a very cold shower. The evenings lately have been Seattle-cold and -rainy. The weather is really preparing me for the Pacific Northwest, head cold and all.

26 July 1967, Wednesday Morning

It's 6:07. We just learned that morning formation will be at 6:30 from now on. That fouls up my whole day's schedule. Time to go to work.

5:15 p.m.

Another unnotable day is drawing to a close. Whether they are interesting or not, they still count on the tour, I know. Today I exchanged five pairs of fatigue pants for ones that fit me. The supply clerk was very disgruntled with me, but I got the pants anyhow, which was the point for the thing. I also got $20 worth of piasters today so now I can get my laundry out of the shop. I've run out of socks and almost underwear, but tomorrow will redeem several bundles. Also I'll drop off five shirts to have labels, name, rank and unit sewed on. That will

give me ten pair of jungle fatigues to wear the last
two and a half months of duty. Rather ridiculous,
but necessary. I hope to look good even more so now
or suffer the consequences.

As you can see from the above material the day
was dull. I sat at my desk most of the day reading
The Crying of Lot 49, which also had some interesting stuff in it on graffiti, which in fact played an
important part in the book as communication.
Modern literature has a thing about writings on
walls, especially latrines. This book by Pynchon was
more readable than *V,* but maybe I'm more recep-
tive now that I've seen more of the absurd and
ridiculous up close, and as a participant.

The sergeant major hasn't yet put up our roster
of details on Sunday, or for the days between now
and then, but I expect I'll be on it and guess I'll
bitch heartily about being included. For all the good
it'll do me.

I've got a gut ache right now, from nervousness,
I guess. Oh, I forgot to type out my R&R form and
must do that now and I will finish this entry later.
I hope the sergeant major doesn't tamper with my
R&R. He's a Machiavellian monster.

9:00 p.m.

I'm in bed listening to the radio. I've been
reading most of the evening, *The Waters Under the
Earth.* It's sort of Lawrence out of Galsworthy and
enjoyable. This evening I also refurbished a fan for
Col. Ebby to have at the office. I've got one for me
there, but he doesn't get much benefit of it. Today
he hinted at that fact by stuffing paper towels up

his sleeves to keep the sweat from trickling onto his desk. Also he's been pestering me for days to bring him an Agatha Christie novel, which I've stuffed in my boot so I shan't forget it tomorrow.

Old Charlie is on his bunk reading *My Secret Life*. He's very moved by it, as I was (a hard-on, I suspect).

It's colder than hell right now, raining (the smell of the outdoor urinal is increased and is very sharp). The weather continues to be very Seattle-ish here.

I guess I'll read a few more minutes and then to bed. Oh yes, Charlie was assigned shit detail for tomorrow and he raised hell about it for a time, and the sergeant major assured him that neither he nor I would have company detail again. When I see it, I'll believe it.

27 July 1967, Thursday Morning

It's 5:55, and I'm about to go to breakfast. This new schedule is all screwed up. Formation is at 6:30, but the lights still come on at 5:30 as before when formation was at 6:00. It don't make sense to me.

That book I'm reading, *Waters Under . . . ,* has a few pages on graffiti too. I can't believe that every modern novel hits that bit, but I guess they do. Also the book mentions a book by Robert Louis Stevenson called *The Wrong Box*. It couldn't be the one from which they got that movie, could it? Probably not. Time to go eat.

12:30 p.m.

Some random thoughts:

Old Joe does miss his sweet little Kathy. And now that they are both together again he's impossible to get along with and gone every night to worship at her throne.

Chow is 1.1 miles away by bus from the office and just about a block from my billets. Convenient, actually. Lamb today for lunch. I wondered what was wrong with the beef 'til I was informed of what it was.

"House of the Rising Sun" must be the most played song over here.

Ed continues to give and charges 25 cents for haircuts.

Old Lt. Col. Rollins and I continue to get along fine. We are both equally difficult customers, and he has a sense of humor that I appreciate even though it's not noticeable to most. Sardonic and sort of persecutive.

Charlie is married and very much in love with his wife. He gets boucoup letters, packages, etc., from her and his family, which I always take as an indication of family solidarity.

The officers here aren't really lecherous. Rollins and Ebby are just healthy, earthy men. Major Tief is the only lecher in the office, and my opinion of him is a low one.

I heard today that this was the longest war we've ever fought, been involved in, or been continuously fighting. I didn't know that!

This place is crawling with earwigs. Earwigs are harmless. They are very old, like roaches, long on Earth, and will be here after the holocaust.

10:15 p.m.

The Red Skelton Show is on. I just watched "The Fugitive." Lt. Gerard has changed his tune. He doesn't think Dr. Kimble is guilty any more. Times change. There's too much racket here tonight. So I'll write more in the morning.

28 July 1967, Friday Morning

It's 6:00 and I'm on my way to breakfast, and Johnny Cash is singing "That Dirty Old Egg Sucking Hound." So it's bound to be a good day.

1:05 p.m.

I don't think I mentioned in my entry yesterday that the sergeant major made up a roster for duty detail in the company and I was on the thing for Sunday, which I expected, as that is the day I'm going to the party. Also the first day off in a long while. I went into the office (admin) and had it out with the sergeant major, so I'm not on the thing, for now anyhow. Smith was his usual genial self. I wonder what he's up to.

Right now everybody is watching an air strike off in the not-too-far distance. Some jets are coming in on a target, dropping their load of fire, and shooting right straight up into the sky, circling around for another hit. The war isn't very far off. I'm glad I'm here and the war is out there.

Kathy just remonstrated with me for not watch-

ing the air strike out of the window, and I replied:
What's the point in watching it if you can't see the
people burning to death? She said well you know
they are bound to be hitting somebody. That's true
enough. Probably not the somebody they intend to
be hitting, though. Maybe I would be more interested in such things if I had the chance to fly over the
area in a helicopter—after the strike is all over, of
course. Maybe one of these days.

I'm glad my bosses won't enforce the rule about
letter writing or reading on the job. I've done both
today and yesterday, and am writing this entry on
the job, with Col. Ebby reading a newspaper. He'd
not buckle under to such an unreasonable request.
Haven't heard boo from the sergeant major, either.

My runny nose is almost gone, my cold is all
gone, and I feel fine, as they say.

Later:

It's 9:05, and I've been reading *The Waters
Under the Earth* since I got home from work. Just
finished it. A good traditional novel — faith in
humanity, fidelity, etc. Will write more in the
morning.

Later Still:

Not morning, but 9:35 p.m. The Youngbloods
were just on TV singing Willie McTell's "Stateboro
Blues"—a good old song that dragged me right out
of bed. Now to bed and sleep.

29 July 1967, Saturday, 6:00 a.m.

I've been listening since about 5:00 to Woody Guthrie's Library of Congress recordings—interview with Alan Lomax, songs, and stories. In 1940 he recorded this. "So Long, It's Been Good to Know You," he's singing. He told about the fires that plagued his family. It's especially sad when one thinks of Woody now sick, and his son Jack dead. It's sad. I'm on my way to mess now.

30 July 1967, Sunday, 9:00 a.m.

It's Sunday. My day off and the day of the party. We leave by bus for the thing at noon.

Last night I got back from the office and dinner at 6:30 and I was showered and asleep by 7:00, to wake at 5:30 when the lights flashed on. And I got up, ate breakfast, returned and was transformed from plodding clerk to plotting poet by reading Auden and Spender, who'd affect any wordsmith that way, I think.

Now Peaches and Herb are singing "Close your eyes, take a deep breath . . ." Sweet thing.

This week was fine because the work was almost zero.

"Black is Black" is now playing. That was big when I left the states some many months ago. "What can I do, cause I'm feeling blue." I actually don't feel blue at all. The time I've got left is but a faucet drip by geologic time.

"What can I do alone with you?" the Mamas and Papas now sing.

I guess I should shave now.

"Woman, do you love me?" Peter and Gordon

now are singing that hit from when I was in basic.

Now the preponderate smell is of Sunday details burning shit (I could be among them, but ain't).

"The Waltz You Saved for Me" by Ferlin Husky. It's request time, so I will shave now.

The green hair net strikes again. —The Bard

10:00 a.m.

I'm shaven and on the way to the big club to have a sandwich with my buddies. A spider just suspended from the ceiling in front of me. A little teeny one reminding me of yester morn.

I walked into work and on the wall was a huge spider with a small body and huge long springy, bouncy legs. I chased him under Major Tief's desk and left him there (In hopes . . .).

But Major Tief didn't come in all day and it crawled out and scared Kathy out of her wits (a good place to be). Lt. Col. Rollins cornered it and stomped it. It sat and bobbed up and down about two inches off the floor on its legs. Quite a sight. Insects should be squashed only if they depart from their part in God's great plan. Or if they cause me discomfort.

"Eat me, Fillipe, I'm a taco bean."
                                  —Dead Head Ed

9:15 p.m.

It's a sunburned soldier that writes these words. This morning I went to the club, had a Coke and bought $1 worth of nickels. I played the slot machines until the bus for the party was to leave. On my last nickel I hit a $3.75 baby jackpot (three dollars seventy-five cents—so came out $2.75 ahead, as I quit and haven't gone back.)

The party was fine, at a boat dock on the Saigon River operated by Army Special Services. I didn't water ski, but went for a speed boat ride I thought would be one more humdrum experience, but not so. As soon as we cross-hit the first rock-solid wave I knew I'd have to use the handle on the dash board or get jarred out into the brown water. I wished the sergeant major would fall victim to the waves when his turn came. But no. He seems blessed with the lives of a cat. The Saigon River is just a public sewer, a perfect resting place for him. The vegetation hits the water solid along the sides, like a mangrove swamp, with brown canals debauching off into the undergrowth. The edges were marked with black and white flags on tall poles, survey markers, I guess.

All I did at the party was eat fried chicken, drink Coke, ogle the Vietnamese girls in bikinis (I did think of my Asian Princess once or twice—she's out of my reach now, forever, I think), and listen to the band. They played "House of the Risin' Sun" among other oldies.

Tomorrow morning at 6:00 we get paid. I'm anxious to see the voucher so I'll know what amount of money we'll be getting.

The latest terror here is a new detail — sandbagging. A huge pile of bags was dumped in front of the barracks. Rumor has it we'll be on detail from 7:30 to 9:30 each night 'til Special Troops is completely sandbagged. Barf, I say. By skill and skullduggery I plan to avoid the whole thing. And if I'm unable to, I know who to blame.

31 July 1967, Monday, 5:45 a.m.

Pay call in fifteen minutes and then I'll write an entry describing the munificent amounts recorded on the voucher.

7:20 a.m.

I'm at the office. I was paid what I expected. One month about 'til I leave for Hong Kong.

> *You talk like man with paper ass hole*
> *—RVN saying*

3:45 p.m.

It's been a big day, and the work still grows and burgeons. Hong Kong is our destination for R&R. We considered Bangkok, but Bangkok's climate isn't much different from what we have here. And it's the change I'm looking forward to. Also Hong Hong is an exciting place to me because it's always mentioned in the spy novels, and I've seen it on "I Spy", etc. Also the English aspect of the pubs, bookshops, and all that stuff attracts me. Also most everybody went to Bangkok when I first got here and now they are going to Hong Kong. One of my buddies who went to Singapore about seven months ago thought it a fantastic place. Seeing these places after being in RVN for six months to a year is much different than seeing them after being in the States, I'm sure. Anyhow, Hong Kong it is, and I know I won't be disappointed. Charlie always enjoys things and isn't a moper or a fellow to delight in being displeased, so I know we'll be pleased with the choice. Now if I were going with Joe or Ed I couldn't be sure of having a good time as they are so different from me.

Speaking of Ed. Some further sagas of Dead Head Ed: Lately, since he returned from Hawaii, he's been wearing a large handsome compass on a leather band on his left wrist. Everyone naturally assumes it to be a watch. When he's asked the time, he solemnly examines its face and silently points north. Good old Ed. He came back from Hawaii with a new toast that is big in the islands: "Suck 'em up." Don Ho uses it all the time. It's used when drinking a certain beer made in the islands, but is very adaptable. Sweatshirted girls are often emblazoned with this comment.

I wasn't kidding about Army latrines being segregated, though if I used an officer's latrine (as I've done due to paper being gone or wet in the EM latrine) nothing is said. Bowels are quietly relieved and that's that. If I used the general's latrine it would be trickier, but I'm sure I could talk my way out of it. Segregation of latrines is funny really. It gives an imaginary feeling that the officers are getting a better deal, but they're not as the latrines are all the same. In every way, even the smell.

I didn't water ski at the office party, although Ed did and swallowed much of the river, and got a hell of a burn. The lieutenant colonel who I went on the speed boat ride with is a fellow who has been in Seattle many times. After we hit the first few

waves, he yelled at me from the back of the boat:
Remind you of Whidbey, specialist? And you know
it did, as that's the only place I've ever had a
similar experience.

The speed boats belong to Army Special Services
and are fine, new fiberglass boats. Many Vietnamese girls over here are very stacked, and it's not
padding, as in a bikini a girl isn't fooling anyone,
especially playing ping pong as these at the boat
dock were. They weren't skinny at all, but one was
very plump. Anthropologically speaking, very interesting. Anthropometrically especially. That sort of
thing has always fascinated me.

1 August 1967, Tuesday, 8:00 p.m.

I'm back in the barracks. Thanks to that shit
Major Tief I had no time to type an entry. He was
finally calmed down by Col. Ebby at 4:45 p.m., but
the day was shot then.

For R&R I'll need a suitcase, new shoes, a
couple pairs of washable dark pants, and a couple of
white shirts. I can't wear fatigues in Hong Kong or
khakis—and that's about all I have.

About the off-loading Army bus procedure—it's
ridiculous, but practical. I kind of dig it because it
is so Army. Martians observing it would think we
are robots. I dig it for the same reason I polish my
brass belt buckle front and back every day.

Today I went to the laundry tailor shop to get
my fatigues back, the new jungles (Dave Clark Five
are singing "You Got What it Takes"—a good song).
Three of my fatigues had the name tags sewn on
upside down. It looked very peculiar. One shirt had

no name tag. Two shirts had Big Red One patches,
rather than USARV. I held them up, said number
10 job, and they quietly took them back. I'll get
them tomorrow and see how they do.

The news is on right now, radio and TV, and I
wish they'd get together as they're hard to understand.

Old Dead Head Ed—this morning the First Shirt
(1st sergeant) personally woke him up. He was the
last man in formation. As the First Shirt called us
to attention, Ed vaulted the ditch and landed in
place. What gall.

The Smothers Brothers just came on. Simon and
whatsis are on tonight. So I guess I'm off to take a
shower.

2 August 1967, Wednesday Morning

It's 5:35 and the Osborne Brothers are singing
and pickin' "Mule Skinners Blues" — "... Hey,
little water boy ..."

Last night when I returned from the shower I
watched the hour long "TW3" and Peter Sellers was
on with a couple of very funny bits. One was of a
long haired wine taster. He had the wine in his
mouth when the camera focused on him. He looked
like he was doing facial isometrics. After very
elaborate facial movements and swallowing, he very
coolly gave the name of the wine, blank 1953. The
interviewer says no, not quite, and off it goes for
about ten minutes 'til he asks, beer? Coca-Cola?
Water? etc. I didn't hear the punch line. Just as on
the "Goon Show", one must have a good ear for
British nuances. I'm a little rusty on my British,

but sharper than ever on southern dialects, white and negro.

Time to put on my boots and trundle off to breakfast. Such as it will be.

6:40 p.m.

I've got a couple of Army stories that I've been meaning to write down but haven't gotten to yet. Here they are.

"The Last Supper"

The first one is from Major Tief's many Eulenspieglenian adventures. He was on an investigation up country on the building of BEQs. Some of these enlisted billets were built in the whorehouse area of this town so naturally Major T. had to check out the area to see what he could see. While there he noticed that one of the shops in this area specialized in life size reproductions of the Playboy Playmates. Framed and very impressive. He bought one and had it wrapped. When wrapped it looked just like a reproduction of The Last Supper.

When he was ready to fly back to Tan Son Nhut he brought the thing out to the airplane and carried it up to the pilot of his plane and explained to him that he had a copy in oil of The Last Supper that he was carrying back to his unit to donate to his unit chaplain for the chapel. Therefore the pilot said that he had a place it could go so it wouldn't get crushed with the other baggage. He could put it on the bunk in the pilot's cabin, and as his Last Supper was going to be up there he could sit up there in the VIP easy chair in the air-conditioned cabin with the pilot.

The rest of the 150 passengers were jammed together on the floor of the unpasteurized freight floor with no seats or anything and were very miserable. So the good major rode in comfort 'til he got back to Tan Son Nhut. When he got to Tan Son Nhut, he gave the same story to a man with a carryall and was driven to his exact destination and given best wishes for his philanthropic gesture. The Last Supper now hangs over his bar in all its splendor. The wages of sin . . .

The second story was told to me by Lt. Col. Rollins yesterday when he was (or maybe the day before) in a story-telling mood and told me stories off and on all day. He's got a lot of good ones and this one is kind of simple, but I enjoyed it as it is illustrative of the puckishness of some Army humor. Entitled:

"The Orangutan"

He knew a very old first lieutenant a few years ago. This lieutenant was very old and had been passed up for promotion. Finally he asked him about it. The lieutenant said that yes, there was a story behind it, and although he used to be very sensitive about, it he was no longer and would be glad to tell about it. It happened back during World War II when he was a young second lieutenant and pilot on an island in the Pacific. Their ritual there, day in and day out, was that about 2:00 every morning the scramble alarm would sound and all the pilots would get dressed, rush out to the field, start up their planes, and get ready to take off. But before that could happen the all - clear always sounded. Now this happened week after week.

Finally the lieutenant got a bright idea. He had a pet orangutan. This was one smart ape. He could do just about anything. So the lieutenant trained the orangutan to respond to the alarm by jumping out of his bed, getting dressed, rushing out to the field, warming up the airplane, and then hearing the all-clear, turning the thing off and returning to his bunk. Now this went on for months and the pilot was leading a fine social life, getting much sleep and way ahead of his peers. One day the whole ritual was gone through, except for the fact that this time the all-clear wasn't sounded. The planes had to take off. Well, the lieutenant said, that's the story of why I'm such an old lieutenant. But, he continued, the thing that really hurts is that damn ape is a lieutenant colonel.

Well, for what they are worth, there they are. The first one could be a short story of the trick ending kind if there was a trick ending, but in life things rarely end trickily, but instead with total predictability. Maybe there is some way that the main character of that piece could get his. I'd like to see him get it, but 'twill never happen.

It's getting on to closing time, so I guess I'll close up and finish this when I get back to the barracks and have showered, etc.

Later:

It's 9:30, and I'm showered and about ready to go to sleep. I spent most of the evening trying to figure out my camera. I bought four rolls of film for it today, put a roll of color slide film in it and shot a

few exposures. Tomorrow I'll finish the roll and
send it off to be developed so I'll have an idea of
how I'm doing and what I have to do to improve. I
expect most of them will be fine.

3 August 1967, Thursday Morning

It's 5:45 a.m. and I'm up and it's Thursday, only
one more day and I'll know for sure whether I get
Saturday afternoon and all day Sunday off. It would
be nice. I could even get caught up in my diary and
read a couple of books straight through instead of
in fits and gasps.

12:40 p.m.

Things have been active here today. Not the
work load, but the shit load. As Lt. Col. Rollins
said: How do I get a transfer out of this chickenshit
outfit. I know Sergeant Major Smith is behind the
bulk of it, but I kept my thoughts to myself. Of
course we are too short to worry, but I'd hate to
have a year ahead of me rather than behind me.
Today we were given a roster of opening up in the
morning, requirements for the signs on our rooms
being six feet, five inches from the floor and two
inches from the door frames, directives on which
items are allowed in a room and which are not,
politeness to visitors, etc. Also a command directive
came down that 25% of the EM staff would be on
sandbag detail every day beginning this morning.
We haven't complied with that last one yet, but I
imagine we will soon. What a dismal outlook to
have if I had just gotten here. At least I can see an

end to it.

Later:

It's 8:30 and I'm back in the barracks. Unshowered as of yet but still plenty of time. If I feel like expending the energy for naught. I say naught because tomorrow I have sand bag detail. Then I work Saturday morning, and have Saturday afternoon and all day Sunday off. Time to recover, although the way I plan to work tomorrow I won't need much recovery time.

My old sergeant major will be working out of our office for the next ten days on a big investigation. He's stationed in Hawaii now. It will be interesting to see him again. We never were boon buddies, but I respected his power and administrative ability. I wish he was still in charge.

"Hold me tight, don't say good-night." Peaches and Herb sing now. A fine song. "Take a deep breath."

Saturday afternoon and Sunday I hope to take some four rolls of pictures to see if I understand my camera.

Today I discussed some Army slang with Lt. Col. Rollins, specifically labels for ranks like colonel—being called 06 (actually a pay grade), bird colonel, chicken colonel, bull colonel, full bull, etc.

For lieutenant colonel there's light colonel, bottle cap colonel, telephone colonel; bottle cap colonel because the rank insignia looks like a bottle cap; telephone colonel because when he answers the phone he says "Colonel Rollins". Fascinating facts, eh? Well, maybe not, but at least peripherally interesting.

4 August 1967, Friday Morning

It's 6:15 a.m. and I'm ready for the big formation. After that I plan to read *The Unicorn Murders*
by Carter Dickson, until 7:30 when the thing
(sandbagging) starts. Charlie has already gone to
work to comply with the new requirement of opening up the office at 6:00 *every* morning. A different
man gets it each morning and the WACs are
exempted. Making coffee and cleaning off desks is
man's work.

> *"Who goes there?*
> *Hankering, gross, mystical, nude;*
> *How is it I extract strength*
> *from the beef I eat?"*
> *—Song of Myself - #20 W.W.*

7:00 p.m.

I'm in the sack, showered, sunburned, and bound
to develop some aches and pains from a vigorous
day of sand-bagging, but feeling fine right now. My
hands are chafed raw, but Ponds Cold Cream has
relieved the burning. Should slow down my typing
and filing tomorrow. God help the sergeant major if
he complains. I told him clerking and sandbagging
are mutually exclusive tasks. He didn't know what I
was talking about.

Another thing—my belly is full of a good meal.
A completely shocking surprise. Everyone in the
mess hall was almost too flabbergasted to eat it.

Steak, baked potato, canned pears, cooked fresh
carrots, chocolate ice cream, iced tea (with ice). All
the food was well prepared and reasonably por-
tioned. An amazing occurrence that is, a one time
thing for sure.

"Journey to the Center of the Earth" with Bat
Poone, James Mason, *et al.*, is the Saturday night
movie, I was just informed by the TV announcer.

"I should have engaged the pigmy witch doctor
when I had the chance. Besides, he could travel for
half fare." Said by Gomez Addams on TV.

Right now the radio is playing "San Francisco
Flowers in Our Hair" or something like that. Very
Mamas and Papas-ish sounding—clear and ballad
sounding.

Now old Bob Dylan is singing "Brand New
Leopard Skin Hat."

I'm now watching riots on TV. These are foreign
but remind me of a remark I heard that there
would be a complete blood bath and armed revolution before there'd be racial equality. Looks like it's
here for sure now. It would be interesting to work
in a city (Seattle soon enough I imagine) aflame
with all that stuff.

Later:

It's 9:35 p.m. and I've been reading the poetry of
Elinor Wylie, which I like very much. I don't find
much poetry to my liking, but hers is fine. Also the
electricity is out. Now it's back on so . . . out the
candle. "Escape"—a small quote from the thing:
"When foxes eat the last gold grape, / and the last
white antelope is killed, / I shall stop fighting and

escape / Into a little house I'll build."

Old Ed just declaimed "Every-day-is-laundry-day-at-Long-Binh-Post." Fine rhythm in that line.

Just overheard from next door where they are having a beer blast that will change for sure our company's policy of allowing beer in the billets. Such raucous caterwauling. "The Army sucks." True, oh, how true.

Dead Head Ed just showed me two books he stole from the library, sober and reportorial—*The Power of Positive Thinking* by Norman Vincent Peale (more than 2 million copies sold) and *How to Stop Worrying and Start Living* by Dale Carnegie. He hasn't read them I don't think. If he has, they haven't affected his "Life Goals" noticeably.

I think I'll go to sleep now and write a bit in the morning.

5 August 1967, Saturday Morning

It's 5:20 a.m. and I'm listening to Woody Guthrie tell the story of Pretty Boy Floyd the outlaw. He's about to sing it too. Didn't that first record I got by Seeger have this one on it? I'm sure it must have. Now he's singing, but I must go shit and get water for shaving. "Deputy sheriff addressed him in a manner rather rude... They say that I'm an outlaw, they say that I'm a thief... Some will rob you with a six gun, some with a fountain pen."

Guthrie is now singing "It takes a worried man to sing a worried song," the version the Kingston Trio made famous with a single "worried," not the doubled "worried, worried" that the Carter Family sold a few million copies of earlier in the century—

1920 something.

Time to eat. Will be back in a few minutes. Woody is singing a song I've not heard before. He's got quite a few I've not heard before.

Well, I'm back and breakfasted. "Searching for My Baby's Love" is playing on the My Lan show. Time for formation.

8:30 p.m.

I got off work at noon today and slept most of the afternoon while half-listening to the Green Bay Packers play all-stars or whatever. I'm listening to Grand Ole Opry. They started off with "It Takes a Worried Man to sing a Worried Song." They just did "Oh Susie-Anna" and are now doing "Nashville Cats." Flatt and Scruggs are performing. A good sound. I think they had a country western hit on the thing — "Pick it, Earl."

A bit of folklore: Bush Books = Cock Books.

Sergeant Major Mills breezed in today TDY from Hawaii for an investigation and only said one thing to me—"How's your Army career?" Fine, I said. He breezed out of the room and an hour later we watched his helicopter take off from the pad outside our window, about half a block away. I hope *one* day I get to ride in one of those whirlybirds.

I think I'll read some poetry. I read *Murder Up My Sleeve* by Erle Stanley Gardner earlier. Maybe some Walt Whitman would be appropriate as an antidote.

6 August 1967, Sunday Morning

It's 9:45 a.m. and "I'm Walking in the Rain" by Del Shannon is on the radio. Today Charlie and I plan to go downtown to Bien Hoa (that muddy string of whorehouses and bars) and take pictures of the suckers standing in lines outside the blow-job parlors. I plan to get a haircut and maybe some python skin cowboy boots if I see any that I like. Now I must go shower and get water for shaving.

7 August 1967, Monday, 7:06 p.m.

I was on detail in the company again today. Sergeant Major Smith doesn't ever try to protect me from company duty. Quite the contrary. The scum. He just says "What can I do" and throws up his hands. I didn't have to fill sandbags or carry them though. The detail sergeant put me in charge of two men and we did odd jobs all day: cleaned latrines, finished the outdoor bulletin board, and dug a few holes. We got an hour and a half for lunch and quit at 5:00. The two men I worked with are both chaplain's assistants and one is an ex-monk. Both are Roman Catholic, and very nice guys to work with. They are very skilled and able at manual labor (I'm not) and we accomplished some good work at our own pace, with nobody on our backs.

Charlie told me that Col. Ebby was very pissed off at having both of his clerks gone today. Kathy was getting compensatory time after being CQ. I guess Col. Ebby said that if he wasn't going to have any clerks, he was going to need two more lieutenant colonels to do the typing and clerical work. I guess I'll have the thing again on Wednesday. I

should have a talk with him about Sergeant Major
Smith. Career men usual stick together though.

Charlie and I got back from Bien Hoa safely. We
just walked up and down the streets (no sidewalks).
A real dump of a town. It's about the same to
Saigon as Drummond, Montana is to Seattle, only
with open sewers. Terrible. My nose almost fell off.

Charlie and I went into a haircut shop. The
cleanliness standards were indescribable (really)
and I expect a case of medieval scrofula to soon
overwhelm me. I found out after the haircut that I'd
paid for a short-time too, but I demurred and sat in
a barber chair and watched the family eat nuoc
mam and rice and have an amusing argument that
culminated in chopsticks being hurled to the floor
and two chairs being knocked about. While I waited,
Charlie got a massage from a girl who obviously
was a short-time girl unskilled in massage.
Throughout her inept massage, Charlie played with
her titties and she kept saying "You fuck me now,"
but he finally fled, triumphantly resistant. He's too
short to take the chance (medical and emotional)
now.

Charlie and I walked up and down the muddy
streets and entered every leather or shoe shop in
town. I bought a python wallet. Also Charlie and I
were measured for custom made cowboy boots in a
cobbler shop; he traced our right feet on a paper,
measured the foot all around. I'm getting a pair of
square-toed, high-topped, high-heeled cowboy boots,
leather-lined, rubber-heeled, in python skin. About
as subtle as a scarlet neon sign, but I wanted them
and will get them next Sunday, if I'm not on detail.

We saw Sergeant Major Smith from a great
distance in a part of town he shouldn't have been. I

wonder what he's up to? I wish we could have taken incriminating photos of him. Maybe he'd lighten our work loads a bit. But no . . .

Scott McKenzie is singing "Flowers in Her Hair". That is a fine song. This evening I've tried to read Agatha Christie's *Peril at End House* but couldn't concentrate on it for a variety of reasons. So I tried to read poetry, Yeats, and the lines ". . . a paltry thing, a tattered coat upon a stick . . ." fit me as my soul doesn't "clap its hands and louder sing . . ." It's easy to get spiritually distressed in such drear, red-clay surroundings as this.

I'll have a Pepsi now and read more Yeats. I'll write more in the morning.

8 August 1967, Tuesday Morning

It's 5:50 a.m. and I'm about to leave for breakfast, in about ten minutes, that is. Last night it rained horizontally again, the rain blowing through the screens on one side of the billets and settling inside on everything and everybody. As usual when I'm exposed to sunlight, yesterday I got a sunburn that is hot across my shoulders and chafes at my collared neck. I guess I'll be back on detail tomorrow and I'll have to wear a shirt for sure.

1:10 p.m.

I'm scheduled for sandbags again on Thursday and for CQ on the 15th of August. While I was gone yesterday, Lt.Col. Rollins did the typing and kept everything caught up so I've nothing extra to do today. Also while I was gone they had the water and phones hooked up. Progress is fine.

> *"It's what you are, not what you got."*
> —*Sonny Bono*

(Rather cryptic don't you think?)

8:25 p.m.

It's evening, of course, and I'm not yet showered or anything but I will, I suppose.

"Close your Eyes, Take a Deep Breath..." Peaches and Herb are admonishing me. I gave my camera to Dead Head Ed (temporarily) so he could learn how to operate it and then teach me. It's beyond me.

Sonny and Cher are on the Smothers Brothers Show. The quote above I got from the Sonny and Cher song.

It's time I'm going to shower as I'm rather smelly. I'll write more tomorrow morning.

9 August 1967, Wednesday Morning

It's 5:55 a.m. and I'm about to go to chow. I woke up to the sound of the Stoneman Family singing "Nashville, Tennessee" accompanied by a jew's harp—boing boing.

Last night I had all kinds of dreams, I think because of this sunburn I've got. I hope it's gone tomorrow when I'm back on detail, and I also have to be at the office to open it up at 6:00. 'Twill be a long day tomorrow, but I don't really mind—I'm too short.

Before I go here's a bit of folklore. Last night late I went out to piss and saw a big old mosquito standing up fucking a turkey against the outhouse. Where the turkey came from . . .

"Ours is not to reason why;
ours is but to read and comply."
— *Army Saying*

10:00 p.m.

Damn Sergeant Major Smith to eternal perdition. Tomorrow I'm again on company detail and hope to get assigned as prisoner guard so I can sit all day with my M-14 and take it easy. I'll probably just end up with the old sandbag detail. It was fun at first, but it's getting to be tiresome.

A Dagwood and Blondie movie is mewling and puking on TV in the background. Dagwood just ran eight or ten miles down the track after a departing train and dragged himself gasping aboard. Silliness triumphant over reality.

The barracks arrangement was changed a bit so two men are in little partitioned cubicles. A bit more privacy.

Blondie just did the trick of smuggling a dog, skillfully camouflaged as a baby, into the passenger car. Ah, triteness, we clutch it as a life-preserver in a life filled with unpredictability (or something).

Today I told Col. Ebby and Lt. Col. Rollins about my custom made python boots I have to pick up Sunday, and their imaginations were beggared and staggered. What could a nice boy like me do with two monstrosities like that in Seattle? I explained

that I'd gotten them so I'd have civilian shoes to
wear in Hong Kong and wouldn't have to wear my
low quarters. They surmised that I'd cause riots
walking into polite society in python skin cowboy
boots. Of course I could cause riots in low quarters
too, so it matters not.

I won't have to go into the office tomorrow to
open up, so will get a chance to doze for a few extra
minutes if I feel so inclined.

Tonight I read a book called *The Deep Blue
Goodbye* by John D. MacDonald. Interesting, but not
a real escape.

It's raining here right now but will most likely
shine as hot as all bloody hell tomorrow. Today
things were slow at the office. Kathy did all the
typing as is usual these days, and I sat behind my
desk trying to keep tabs on my suspense system,
file my cases, do my monthly report, and reassemble
all the stuff Kathy screwed up. A slow boring day
with few highlights. Lt. Col. Rollins and Col. Ebby
were, as always, cynical and efficient and enjoyable
as superiors. If I had bosses like that as a civilian,
things would be pleasurable at work.

It's 10:35 and time to sleep.

10 August 1967, Thursday Morning

It's 5:50 and it rained all night, so sandbagging
today will be nigh impossible as it raineth still and
the land is puddled up and peaking through only in
high places. For once I do have my raincoat here
when I need it. One of those small consolations, for
otherwise I feel punchy and out of fettle, a way I
get toward the end of the week.

I work tomorrow afternoon so my only hope for time off is Sunday, which seems likely, all things considered. It's about time to drag up to the mess hall for that good old re-up chow.

6:50 a.m.

Formation is just now over and the only memory of chow is a slight feeling of indigestion. Old Ed was the last one to make the formation this morning. I can't understand the reason for it. I guess that everyone can't get by on six hours of sleep, and I too look forward to being back where I can sleep in late without fear of reprisal.

Sunday will be the big day. At that time I'll have only *69* days left! Charlie's now leaving for the office.

9:20 p.m.

I spent the day carrying sandbags and taking breaks, each about equal in time to the other. Nonetheless I'm quite tired this evening and don't look forward to a Friday and a Saturday in the office and an almost certainty of a detail in the company on Sunday, which would almost cause me for sure to lose my python skin boots. Expect the worse and you won't be disappointed, especially where Sergeant Major Smith is concerned.

Today sandbagging was almost manic. We tried carrying the things on our heads as do the gooks. It panicked them. As with most things we do, they immediately saw the humor.

Effective tomorrow, Army uniform must be worn

in the mess hall, command building, and almost
everywhere else. If one changes out of dirty uniform
at the end of long dirty day, it must be into a clean
uniform if one has yet to eat. The Army wishes to
pervade every moment of our lives. I look forward
to escaping it for a few days on my R&R.

Mike D. is leaving on his second R&R in a few
days. He too is going to Hong Kong. He leaves first
week of September. He's one of the few stenos in
country who I knew in Fort Ben, because my
Italian adventure threw things off. At this time he
works in the office across the street from my billets.
I wonder how the others fared over here? As well as
I, or worse? Maybe even better, although I suspect
not. A few will get bronze stars, but as the bard
said, "It don't show on your pay voucher."

I guess I'll climb into my different sheets and
sleep now.

11 August 1967, Friday, 6:00 a.m.

I'm running behind schedule this morning. I've
already received intimations that today will be a
loser. I've had trouble adjusting to the cramped
conditions of a barracks, specifically living out of an
Army footlocker. My fingers are covered with little
infected cuts that I get trying to open the goddamn
thing. This morning I had a particularly difficult
time, so when I got what I wanted out of the thing
I slammed the lid down violently. A few minutes
later I opened the lid. The top of my locker was
filled with white shaving foam from a large aerosol
can that I'd jammed open. Rather funny if it
happens on TV. That took me a while to clean up.

Now I don't know if I'll be my usual cheerful self in the office. I'll just have to keep a stiff upper lip, I guess.

Time to try to fit in breakfast. I'll write more later.

Later: Just had breakfast and made formation. Now to work.

5:15 p.m.

I saw a guy from Yakima today, by name of Madden, whose father owned the ice cream place at the corner of 16th and Nob Hill. He works in this building somewhere.

Some notes on the Army situation here:

Lt. Col. Rollins has no command authority over me in my company. He's just my immediate boss at work. The office and the company are separate. The company gives me details (sandbagging, guard, KP, all of that.) Lt. Col. Rollins has naught to say about it. They (Col. Ebby and Lt. Col. Rollins) are entirely separate from my company which is run by a 26-year-old lieutenant. With a high school education. Only Sergeant Major Smith is in a position to help me, and I know better than to expect that.

These details are for all of Special Troops, which is broken down into companies, my company being Administration. In the lines of authority, Col. Ebby has authority over all officers lower (junior) to him —lieutenant colonels, majors, etc. No matter where they are. Lt. Col. Prince, Lt. Col. Rollins and Col. Ebby don't run a democratic system of leadership, but one of benevolent and informed autocracy. I prefer it that way.

I'm completely protected from outside forces by their power, except for the company, of course, and that's a big exception. I have more power than most lieutenants (even though I'm a lowly SP5) because I work for a colonel who uses me as his agent, giving me full power of a colonel. More than any lieutenant, except one who works for a general. Col. Ebby is a full-bull 0-6 bird colonel, and Lt.Col. Rollins is a bottlecap colonel.

I read in an old Seattle paper today Emmett Watson's comment: We are losing both Vietnam and Detroit, and the battles are interrelated. Many negroes go home from Vietnam with a conviction that things by God better improve, and they have the violence to do something about it.

Riots aren't fun, but anarchy should produce a more equal situation in the cities. I think I'll enjoy working in a social situation of flux, especially if I go into urban social work of some kind.

8:00 p.m.

We have a passive alert in six minutes. The lights go out and we stay on the ground (floor) until it's over. I hope it's over quick. I listened to "Ode to Billie Joe" and liked it—ethnic. It sounded funny on 50 cycles instead of 60, but that's life. I hope to listen to it again when I've got a good record player available from a guy who gets back from R&R in a couple of days.

It's 9:00 and I just watched "Gun Smoke." I'm now about to go to bed. I just drank a Pabst Blue

Ribbon and am very drowsy.

12 August 1967, Saturday, 5:55 a.m.

I'm listening to old Woody Guthrie tell a dust bowl story and sing "Dust Pneumonie Blues," "California Blues," "Tom Joad's Ballad" — "I'm goin' where the water tastes like wine. I'm going where the water tastes like wine. You know? That Georgia water tastes like turpentine."

Now he's singing "Dust Bowl Refugees." Some of his songs he's accompanied with an almost Furry Lewis sound. These Dust Bowl songs he's accompanying with a simple, almost clumsy strum.

9:20 p.m.

Tomorrow I don't work or have detail and will be able to pick up my python boots. Charlie got his black cowboy boots today and they are fine ones that fit him perfectly. I'm going downtown (Bien Hoa) in the morning and will return promptly for the company party in the afternoon—steak and all that stuff.

A guy who came into the office a few weeks ago, named Don, is going downtown with me. Col. Ebby is trying to get him as my replacement so I'll have plenty of time to train him. He's a good guy. Weird as anybody. He combs his hair 24 hours a day. Even in his sleep. Honest to God.

Work today was uneventful and calm. Kathy did the work and I presided at my desk in the outer office. I'm too short to work. Tomorrow is the big day #69.

My sunburn is peeling, in little spots. I think I'll
go to sleep now after reading "Some Rhymes of a
PFC."

13 August 1967, Sunday Morning

It's 7:10 and I'm about ready to do downtown to
get my boots. No breakfast this morning as it's too
much trouble to put on fatigues and then change
into mufti again to go downtown.

I'm going to shave now. And today I *will* learn
how to use that camera of mine. Maybe I'll get
some interesting and useful pictures, depending on
who we run into of course.

7:20 p.m.

I went downtown to Bien Hoa today with Dead
Head Ed and Don. We drug through half the bars
and whorehouses in town, taking pictures and in
general irritating the hell out of the populace. We
didn't spend any money, of course. I took three rolls
of film with my camera and got pictures of all kinds
of interesting stuff: the guy who sprays DDT, all
kinds of whores, bar girls, babies with their fathers,
monks, monkeys in trees, fortune tellers, pool play-
ers, wheel gambling. And yes, a couple of distant
shots of Sergeant Major Smith, up to God knows
what.

I went to the cobbler shop and my boots are in-
progress — a-work, as was *Finnigan's Wake.* I'll go
downtown Wednesday and see if they are done.

Smothers Brothers are on the radio doing the bit
about "My old man's an anthropologist, what do you

think about that?"

The python skins looked good. He had trouble getting them, he said, but would certainly finish them by Wednesday. Tuesday night I have CQ and have compensatory time off the next day for sleep lost. So I'll go down and get the things.

Dead Head Ed was in fine form today. Kids love him, and we took dozens of kid pictures as they'd do all kinds of mugging around to please him. He's been in a real story-telling mood lately. Told stories about hitchhiking cross country in uniform with his hat emblem held on with bubble gum, as he'd lost the nut to the bolt.

Also a story about his first whorehouse experience at Fort Polk. The pimp was reading a comic book and holding a 45 in his right hand. The girl (a Creole "negro") dropped her pants to her knees and flipped up her dress and that was that. Ed paid his money and left. No service performed.

Today we followed every 8-year-old boy who told us he had "numbah one girl — sucky-fucky." Not one number one girl did we see. Some number three or four, through the rice powder on their faces.

One theme here is child labor. Countless examples of children working (*hard*) did I immortalize on celluloid—little girls doing beadwork; kids digging, selling, pimping. Often their elders are hanging around watching.

Ed just opened his mail, a bank statement saying he has a balance of ten cents. Five months now. He looks on it as his contribution to the ultimate downfall of capitalism. All the paperwork, costing them so very much money.

I took two rolls of black and white today and will have them developed. I need money. All I have

left is money to pay for those boots. And I'm getting
anxious about R&R money.

The party today wasn't much, of course, but the
chicken, steak, potato salad, etc. were fine and I
was very hungry.

Oh yes, a postlude to Ed's story about the whore.
After being with her the short, unsuccessful time,
he got a red bump on his dick. He told his sergeant
and the sergeant made many jokes about Ed's
whoring, etc. Ed went to the doctor. "No, I didn't
use no rubber; no, I took no precautions." The bump
was examined and found to be a spider bite.

Another alert is scheduled for tonight. The
whole company is half drunk. I slept through the
last two and plan to do the same tonight.

I've soaked up all of Vietnam that I wish to,
with one large exception, the undropped shoe being
Mme. Ky, my unrequited love. And I am getting
more and more anxious to get home. Sixty-nine days
is short, wouldn't you say? They can keep me in
Oakland for a while before I'm separated, but not
long, I hope. I guess I'll read for a while now,
maybe get a 7-Up from out front.

14 August 1967, Monday, 6:20 a.m.

I've not eaten breakfast. Formation is in a few
minutes. I'm listening to My Lan nauseate her way
through a prelude to some crappy song.

We had the alert last night from 1:00 to about
2:30. Cut the heart right out of my sleep. I feel fine
yet, but I'm sure it won't last. I won't get to the
office 'til about 7:30 this morning. This rigid
schedule is enervating. I look forward to a bit of

sleeping in and an ignorance of what time it is. Time for formation.

"California is the only state that has oranges that suck back."

—*Dead Head Ed*

9:35 p.m.

It's almost time to go to sleep. Another passive alert is scheduled for tonight. It's raining outside and the wind blows. I have my raincoat hung around the end of my bed to keep away the spray of rain that comes through the screen.

Today was a very busy day. Old Kathy (her nerves afflicted by the curse of her monthlies) left early this morning, so I had the Monday bitching to myself. Also the good Major Tief was in the office and he harassed me all day about the "mood" he thinks I'm in. Actually I'm in a good humor, considering. My pleasures are much fewer here than at Tan Son Nhut, and not nearly so frequent. No library to hide in and no time to hide anyhow. And no romantic focus, not even fantasy. Instead I brood about Sergeant Major Smith and what he'll be up to next.

Not much of moment is happening to me of late, and I'm tired so I guess I'll go to sleep, 'til the alert, anyhow.

15 August 1967, Tuesday, 6:00 a.m.

No alert last night so I got a good night's sleep. Now I'm listening to Flatt and Scruggs singing

"Nashville Cats." And I'm off to breakfast.

11:55 p.m.

I am at the orderly room on CQ, so I'll type some comments on my war.

I hear Bob Dylan very often over here. Lately it's "Leopard Skin Pill Box Hat." A hit in the States, I think. At least it was. I'm glad to hear he's making a record. I'd read that he broke with Columbia.

Why do we have a marching band here anyway? For morale of course. This is hardly a hardship area. It's just like any place in the States, and they all have bands. I think it nonsense, but a band is fine I guess. All the band guys do is band. They travel quite a bit to Japan, etc.

Tomorrow afternoon I go after my boots and I'm sure they will be ready and fine. I'll have to scrape up a few piasters for transportation, but have most of the money saved away for the boots.

Don and the Goodtimes are now singing: that Pacific Northwest sound.

Today the Nha Trang team arrived and Dave C. and Traywick are now living here. Traywick leaves in 30+ days so is quite elated and looks forward to getting home to his pregnant wife. (He had an emergency leave.)

Speaking of earwigs: I was ordered to step on a huge one in the hall today and did so with dispatch and efficiency.

My CQ runner just came back from head count in the mess hall and he's now going to sleep. I'm going to stay up all night, and then sleep in the

morning and go downtown about 2:00 or so. To get
my PYTHON BOOTS.

TV reception is fine here, much better than in
Saigon and about as good as in the better parts of
Seattle, not down in a hole or behind a hill.

The fellow who might be my replacement is a
funny fellow. Don. He's a worshipper of Hank
Williams, not because it's the thing to do, not at all.
At first when he told me his record collection
consisted almost solely of Hank Williams records, I
just assumed that he had them because it was sort
of camp and the thing to do.

Since then I've realized that he's really involved
with the Hank Williams ethic and he quotes lyrics
often with great familiarity, and they sound very
good and like modern poetry and like good stuff. I
can't quote from any one poet very extensively,
except maybe Dylan, and sketchily there. But he
has a Hank Williams quote on every subject.

I've not seen a movie for a long, long time and
will love seeing the things again in 60+ days. The
Dirty Dozen was a very good book, I'm told, and the
movie I'd enjoy, I know, as it's been criticized for its
bloodiness. Also I look forward to John Wayne and
Robert Mitchum—those good old guys.

"All you need is love, love is all you need," by
the Beatles is on, and it's simple and a good song.

The detail of cleaning latrines is a relief from
typing all day. Dead Head Ed accepted the detail
permanently 'til he DEROSs just to avoid the office.

It's 3:15 now, and my mind has stopped working
with any smoothness, so I'll stop writing.

"All you need is love
Love is all you need." —The Beatles

16 August 1967, Wednesday, 7:15 p.m.

The bit above I just heard for the second or third time. That's a fine incantatory prayer of a song.

Today I slept most of the day, didn't pick up my boots, wrote, showered, and I feel great.

Bob Dylan is now singing "Pill Box Hat."

I have Saturday afternoon off and will pick up my boots then, unless things go awry. I think I'll go to the club and get a Coke, etc.

17 August 1967, Thursday, 5:45 a.m.

The Stoneman Family is singing "Back in Nashville, Tennessee" accompanied by a jew's harp. A nice waker-upper. Snooky Lanson has a live TV show in Texas? A small bit of knowledge from the radio. About as valuable a bit as it ever gives out with.

Time for me to go eat, after I polish my belt buckle, front and back. Oh yes, last night we popped popcorn, and I ate my share.

9:00 p.m.

Today was an easy-going day. I went to the laundry to get my film back. I'd lost my receipt of course, and they said no tickee, no pickees—which I didn't go for. I asked them if anybody else had ever lost his receipt and apparently I'm the first one. Tomorrow they'll have them for me, I'm sure. They

won't want to witness another tantrum like the one
I threw today when after not finding my pictures
they then didn't give me the change from my
laundry. They did finally, of course.

Tomorrow evening I can go to a party an NCO
in the office is throwing at the Senior NCO Club
because he made sergeant major. Steak and booze. I
burn garbage tomorrow, so I'll be tied up with that
'til about 8:00. It's been taking three hours of late
to burn the garbage. That's not reasonable.

I've read a few pages of Patchen's *Memoirs of a
Shy Pornographer,* and it's better than many books
that do similar things written since.

18 August 1967, Friday Morning.

It's 5:45 a.m. and Roger Miller is singing "Doo
Wacka Doo." Charlie and I got our numbers on the
flight manifest to Hong Kong. I'm #1 on the list;
Charlie is #3, out of 53. We get our positions by
time in country since last R&R out of country. I've
got almost a year as of 3 September, the day I
leave.

Yesterday our section learned we were to be
consolidated into a smaller area of rooms. So Kathy
and Tief will be moved into our room. Ugh, those
ugly mugs won't be a pleasing couple of things to
look at. I can feel the ham-like hand of Sergeant
Major Smith in this change. But I'm too short to be
bothered. I'm going to eat now.

6:25 a.m.

I'm back from chow, such as it was.

11:00 p.m.

I went to the party, had steak, chicken, beans, fresh pineapple, potato salad, etc. Fine dinner. Good steak even. It seemed like a million people were there. I got there late, of course, because Dave C. and I got lost trying to find the place. It's about a two-minute walk from my barracks.

Everyone from our section was there. Major Tief, putting whiskeys down like mad. I was telling stories about my unsuccessful attempt yesterday to get my pictures from the gooks' laundry. He was good-natured about it and finally said that he couldn't take it all day and all evening too.

Tomorrow I am going downtown to get my boots. Also to take more pictures. I wish I knew if my last three rolls came out. On Sunday I work all day, but hope not to do much.

Time for bed.

19 August 1967, Saturday Morning

"When first to this country, a stranger I did come . . ." The New Lost City Ramblers are singing that fine song. It's 5:45 and I woke up late this morning.

Oh, yesterday I got three shots in my right arm, and it dearly smarts today. Time for me to piss, shave, etc.

Later: Leadbelly just sang "Rock Island Line." Now Eve Darling is doing "Swanoa Tunnel," the Bascom Lamar Lunsford song. I've eaten, and now to formation and then to work.

9:15 p.m.

Here I am, all showered and recovered from my
trip to Binh Hoa with Dead Head Ed. Today I came
into the barracks after lunch to go downtown with
Ed. I couldn't find him. I asked Traywick if he saw
him. He didn't. I walked over to the mamasan's
corner where she was polishing boots. With her was
a papasan I identified as Ed. He'd been there most
of the morning without anybody noticing he wasn't
Vietnamese. He was stripped to the waist and had
on a cone hat that concealed his face, and he was
squinched down right close to her. He wouldn't even
talk to me. Later I discovered he'd been playing sex
games with her for hours. I thought the atmosphere
was peculiar.

Downtown he found a little monkey of a soft
drink seller who appealed to him, and he disappeared down an alley with her for an hour and a
half while I sat on the corner and refused to sell my
wrist watch and camera to 10-year-old pimps who
wanted to buy. I also took a few pictures.

I got my boots today and am very pleased with
them. They are very snakey looking. I also got a
snake belt with a big chrome buckle. I also got my
black and white pictures back today—37 out of 40
came out. Some are very good. The shots of Sergeant Major Smith are so distant it could be
anybody—the man in the moon or Sergeant Bilko.
Too bad. Maybe next time.

The shot I like best is of the man with the pole
across his shoulder with all the little leaf-wrapped

packages. Second, Ed and a bunch of kids with wholesome gestures. Ed always brings out the best in children.

Third, Ed and a straw-hatted cyclo driver with nasty dental problems. Fourth, the bug spray man, a man of dignity and a squint. Fifth, four little kids engaging in business, purchase of a RVN delicacy sold by children to children. I'll get better with practice, I'm sure. I'm going to take color slides in Hong Kong, but only black and white in Vietnam. They are more revealing than slides, I think, and much cheaper. My main problem in the black and whites I took is my focus. I had on dark sunglasses and couldn't tell when I'd reached focus. Today I took them bare-eyed and hope for improvement.

Today I took pictures of drawings on alley walls, construction, the food vendors, and whatever struck my fancy.

Tonight I have the August *Playboy* to read. It's not very interesting. My books are much more enjoyable.

Tomorrow Ed and I are clerks on duty. I plan to do very little work. I hope to read *Memoirs of a Shy Pornographer.*

Charlie and I got our notice that we can pick up our R&R orders 1 September. We leave the Second for Ton San Nhut, from whence Hong Kong. Unless things go wrong.

My boots are a triumph of cobblery. I'd love to have taken pictures of the cobbler working on them in his medieval sweatshop, staffed almost exclusively by child labor, but the place was much too dark.

Today Ed and I tried to take pictures of a knife sharpener, an evil old man with a wickedly long knife. He kept brandishing it. Ed and I dodged and ran, but returned 'til finally we got our pictures.

Binh Hoa is so dirty I'm even hesitant to drink bottled Coke. And I'm not usually cautious. I don't plan to return. We didn't catch even a glimpse of Sergeant Major Smith.

Tomorrow I'll take my camera to work and photograph the headquarters, the huge machines, and anything else I like.

I'm going to read for a while now and then to sleep.

20 August 1967, Sunday Morning

It's 5:50 and I'm about to go to chow. No formation on Sundays, but of course the lights still come on at 5:30. The Brothers Four just came smoothly on to the radio waves, singing "Midnight Special." They are no Leadbelly, not even four of them. By the way, all of the Leadbelly Library of Congress recordings are going to be played on the folk show on early Saturday mornings, the same one on which I heard the Woody Guthrie recordings for three consecutive Saturdays. "There's Whiskey in the Jar." "I'd like to see my brother, the one that's in the Army," they now sing. I guess he's going to play their whole album.

Time to go for breakfast.

"A hoard of millions of mice swept across wide areas of Bosnia Wednesday . . ."
                              —just heard on the radio

8:50 p.m.

Things are bad all over the world, but it can't be helped, I guess. How's that for an attitude for a future architect of social change?

Today was a slow one down in the office. All I did all day was sit and watch the rain hit the heavily oiled blacktop of the square. I watched it 'til the water appeared to be bubbling out of the blacktop.

Another thing I did today was listen to Major Tief expound his foolproof method of winning $2700 at roulette in the gambling casinos of Hong Kong. Two hours it took, diagrams and all. I guess I will try it, cautiously, and just for the fun of losing $10 or so. Also I'll have to visit an opium den. That'll be fun.

I think Charlie and I will stay at the Hong Kong Hilton, $6.50 per room per day. We'll decide when we get there. The food will be Chinese most of the time if I have my way. And I think I will.

I typed for about four minutes today. What a dull day. Maybe I'll ask for tomorrow afternoon off to rest up.

"Ba Ba Barbara Ann" by the GREAT Beach Boys—a fun incantation in fine harmony from the Beach Boys Beach Party album. Now Johnny Cash's ode to his woman's pudendum—"Burning Ring of Fire." "Teen Angel" — I remember that tearful dedication to the dead—"Are you somewhere up above? And are you still my one true love?"

I heard an album of Buddy Holly and the Crickets the other day. He had a fine sound. I'll have to get an album of his, too.

I look forward to reading tomorrow while Kathy

types all the junk that came in today. Unless she
goes on sick call again. Only three times last week
did she pull that shit.

I've been reading *Paterson* now and again and
think it a weird book, akin in a strange way to *The
Sotweed Factor*. Only it's a history of New Jersey—
Paterson, New Jersey.

Time for bed, 9 before 10. I'll write a bit in the
morn.

21 August 1967, Monday, 5:50 a.m.

This morning I didn't jump out of bed the
moment the alarm went off as I usually do. Age
must be finally catching up with me. I don't feel
chock full of energy. Ah well, maybe that fine Army
chow will revitalize me. I think that what I need
won't be stuck between the fried eggs and bacon on
the brown plastic Army tray. If it is, I'll be
gabberflasted, as that country bard would say. I'm
on my way.

5:30 p.m.

I've been reading the temperatures of Seattle in
the *Stars and Stripes,* and it's unseasonably hot
there. We could use it here. When I take that cold
shower I get chilblains between the shower house
and the billet. A cold wind and often hard pelting
rain. At night it's especially chill.

Today was an easy day. Kathy fell down some
stairs, she says, and I'm sure she did and has
quarters 'til Wednesday. So I'm alone with the tiny
burden. And that's what it is. Today I helped Col.

Ebby with his crosswords (he's much better than I am) and watched the machines in the square do their blacktopping.

9:25 p.m.

Do I contradict myself? For tonight I went to a movie starring Victor Mature and Peter Sellers. Not much of a movie, but Sellers had some good bits, and Mature was fine, but then he's always been a fine actor. He was both slapstick and satirical, and even a bit touching a time or two. Vittorio De Sica directed. "After the Fox" was the title, and it was color.

Tonight it's very chilly and I feel a slight sore throat.

Today I saw a security propaganda poster put out by the U.S. Army. It was a large picture of Donald Duck from the shoulders up, and it was captioned something like this: "BE CAUTIOUS, HE MAY BE A COMMIE SPY!!" Totally serious, this is what they do with our tax money.

I'm off to sleep now.

22 August 1967, Tuesday, 5:50 a.m.

Though the rains may fall, our skies will all be blue... Sayeth the radio. I believe it. Time to go eat.

> *Mary had a little lamb,*
> *And when she saw it sicken*
> *She shipped it off to Packingtown*
> *And now it's labelled chicken.*

8:20 p.m.

Bob Dylan is singing "Leopard Skin Pill Box Hat."

Vietnam is a fine place to have been, as a soldier. It's the place to be a civilian (Dept. of the Army Civilian). They are getting rich. I could bank fifteen to twenty thousand tax free dollars over here in eighteen months as a civilian employee. It's true.

Dave Clark Five now singing "You've Got What it Takes." Yeah!!

About Dead Head Ed, he's never stable and sensible. Not in the accepted sense. He is responsible, though, in a weird way. One thing he is all the time—a fine, good person. A good friend and less of a hypocrite than most anybody. It would be fine with me if he lived in Seattle. His head is filled with weird stories. But I think that's true of all of us.

It's not long 'til I'm home, one month and days (29 of them). I won't mourn the Army regimentation, though I need it here as there is nothing else to structure my life. Things go faster with all the bullshit. Remember, WETSU! (We Eat This Shit Up)

I guess I shook off that sore throat, though I have yet to shower.

I was talking to Ed about the story of his sticking his metal emblem on his hat with bubble gum. And he said that actually it worked fine, except the weather was very warm and when he leaned over, the thing hung down a few inches on a string of pink bubble gum. So he'd have to stick it back on. Good old Ed.

What's purple and illegal? — Statutory Grape.

I really do hope that Kathy will be at work
tomorrow so I can take the afternoon off and catch
up on my reading. Somebody up there likes her; I
wonder who?

Time for a shower and bed.

23 August 1967, Wednesday, 5:55 a.m.

Well, today I might have the afternoon off. Odds
are 50-50 Kathy will stretch her quarters 'til
tomorrow, so I must be strong and accept the
possibility of working all day today. Nope, I can't
accept it. And I'll get even if I have to.

Time to go eat. And then to that formation.

Oh yes, the DAC in our office, the middle-aged
negro secretary, just returned from R&R in Hong
Kong, and she said it was peaceful and there was
no way to tell where the headlines were coming
from. She had a ball there, she said.

4:50 p.m.

I've had the afternoon off and got much done. I
got a haircut and massage in one of the Army
mobile barber shops—air conditioned, too. Very
luxurious.

Old Ed just brought me an opened Coke. "Dedi-
cated to the One I Love" is playing. A beautiful
song still.

Charlie just told me I have guard (bunker) on 30
August. It's no big deal, but I get the next day off,

payday. That makes me happy, as I'll have time to buy some junk I'll need for R&R.

24 August 1967, Thursday Morning

It's 5:50 a.m. and it's another day adownin'. I went to sleep early last night. Just three more days 'til I get a day off. I work Thursday, Friday, Saturday all day each day, but get Sunday off. Time to go eat, and then formation.

9:15 p.m.

I've spent the evening watching Thomas play the pinball machines and writing. Also today Major Tief and Kathy moved into our room, so we're now all one big happy whatever. Relationship storms are a-brewin'. Tonight my ex-monk friend read to me crucial entries from his spiritual diary and showed me pictures of him and his fellows in their habits, or cowls, or whatever.

There is no shower water tonight, so I won't waste any time out there. "The Fugitive" is on right now, half over, and Thomas is telling Dead Head Ed the entire story ending and all.

I've been looking at some of the pictures I took in town, including one of a restaurant on a sidewalk in an alley. The soup looked good, but I'm too suspicious to try any. The sanitary conditions in the street eateries in which only Vietnamese eat prove the Vietnamese lack of belief in the germ theory of disease. Dishes are rinsed in cold water, not washed with soap or hot water, no sterilization. Flies swarm unnoticed. Meat sits in the open, unrefrigerated. Terrible. That's why almost 98% of the Vietnamese have body parasites of some kind—internal ones, worms of all varieties. I wish we'd seen the sergeant major. Maybe next time.

25 August 1967, Friday, 5:30 a.m.

Another day. No water except some in a tote can. Glen Campbell is singing "Too Late to Worry, Too Late to Cry." I remember when he was doing the folk-rock thing. He's back solid in the country-western vein again.

Time to shave my face.

8:00 p.m.

Today was not a bad day. I spent most of the morning changing our office around, desk arrangement, and the afternoon helping Lt. Col. Rollins move his stuff from his old BOQ to his new BOQ, and the evening burning trash. I typed one letter today, a personal one for Col. Ebby.

Sunday I'm going downtown and take many people on celluloid. Today I looked at all of Ed's pictures. He took them when we were downtown last weekend. About 50 or 60 of the finest black and white pictures I've seen. Ed has the knack of taking pictures of people, especially children, so they are very alive-looking. Also his pictures of walls are fine. Every picture looks like a prize winner.

I saw somewhere that Kennewick is mighty hot —105 degrees. It's 20 degrees cooler here.

Dead Head Ed gave me a lighter with the engraving: "As I walk through the valley of the shadow of death, I shall fear no evil, for I'm the meanest motherfucker in the valley."

Time to read some Randall Jarrell and then early to bed, for tomorrow will be a long day.

26 August 1967, Saturday Morning

It's 6:15 and I'm shaved and have eaten, with naught to say. One week from tomorrow and I'm off on R&R. When I get back I'll be very short. Time to form up.

> *"The nakedness of woman is the work of God."*
> *Proverbs of Hell—Blake*

7:00 p.m.

A library has been opened up in the building I work in. This I discovered when I went to look up something for Col. Ebby. Lately he's been trying to figure out what narcotic effect betel nut has. Also he spends all his spare time reading Webster's 3rd International.

Anyhow, the library is exclusively new paperbacks of the "cultural" type. I checked a couple to see if English romantic poetry had improved lately. It hadn't. Blake is very fine as always. The others aren't worth a damn. A good line here and there, but that's all. Read his "The Mental Traveller."

Today I read of the assassination of George Lincoln Rockwell. A terrible thing. One of our nation's great bigots dead. A man who was needed, I think, to show the insanity of racial hate. Yet a man with wit and intelligence in contrast to the uppy-ups of the KKK.

Lots of election time action in Saigon. I'm happy to be in dull old Binh Hoa. Charlie and I are going in with Dead Head Ed tomorrow. Ed leaves Monday ETS for Oakland. So tomorrow will be farewell. We'll miss him greatly. I hope to see him again.

I take back what I said about the Romantic poets. There's Keats. He can't be left out. "Though you should build a bark of dead men's bones / and rear a phantom gibbet for a mast, / Stitch shrouds together for a sail, with groans / To fill it out, bloodstained and aghast . . ." from "Ode on Melancholy." Good stuff, and manly. Of course there are a couple of good poems by Thomas Lovell Beddoes— "Resurrection Song" and "The New Cecilia." I forgot Coleridge too. I can see now that I spoke too hastily. There are several good ones.

Grand Ole Opry just came on and it's 8:05. Grandpa Jones is singing a song about Daylight Savings Time. Great funny stuff, Banjo accompanied. "I'd a hung that man who first thought up daylight savings time."

Flatt and Scruggs are now picking and singing a song about old mother. "It's only the wind—Your children are not at the door."

Skeeter Davis is now singing "I'm goin' down the road feeling bad."

I'm going to sleep now as it will be a tiring day tomorrow, dragging up and down the alleys of Binh Hoa. Even the main streets are alleys.

27 August 1967, Sunday, 9:50 p.m.

I'm watching "Bonanza."

Today Charlie, Joe, Ed, and John and I went downtown and took pictures, while also celebrating Ed's leaving. Ed got very drunk and wouldn't come back to the headquarters with Joe, Charlie, and me so we left John with him as watchdog. Ed left the bar he was in with John, alone, and much later John got hold of him again—minus his watch, keys, and all torn up and beaten by five hooligans.

Ed is right now passed out on his bed as he has been for five hours. He drank most of a fifth of vodka today and three beers put him out of his mind. Tomorrow morning he has an awards ceremony for which we hope to have him prepared.

The Turtles just sang their two recent hits, on The Ed Sullivan Show. Now he has some crazy dancers in masks yelling and jumping around. The Devil take them.

Today's trip to downtown Binh Hoa wasn't really very much fun, not only because Ed got fucked up, but because I ran out of film and didn't then have any real point in being there. Also John and I got a verbal reprimand from some MPs for being in an off-limits alley. No big deal, but it cast a small pall on the day. The alleys aren't marked and neither are the streets, but if one is fairly sober and not rowdy it's nothing.

One thing that happened that was of interest was that we spotted Sergeant Major Smith skulking around in the same off-limits area we were in. We think he didn't see us. We caught sight of him from afar, so we think we know something about him he doesn't know about us. We conjecture that he was up to something nefarious, probably a stashed-away underage girl, or maybe a boy. I wouldn't put it past him. That slimy bastard.

Today I decided my python boots are too small,
that is the right one. And I can't wear one boot.
They are about 9½, and I need larger. I'm going to
get some sandals in Hong Kong, so my toes can
breathe. The best laid plans . . .

Time for bed.

28 August 1967, Monday, 6:15 a.m.

I'm tired. Old Ed woke up this morning at 3:30
and then woke me up to open a coke for him. I'm
tired but soon old Ed will be gone and I'll get
boucoup of that.

Ed just walked up singing "Let's go surfing now,
everybody's learning how . . ." wearing a red canvas
cowboy hat and black shorts. I just broke open his
lock for him. He still can't find his keys. I guess
they must be permanently gone.

10:15 p.m.

Naught to say tonight. Ed left today in real
Dead Head style — in fine humor, his face all
scratched from barbed wire, his left cheek-bone
ripped open. He almost lost an eye yesterday, but
not quite—as usual.

I've been reading American poetry most of the
evening, except for an article in *Fortune* on J.C.
Penney. I've decided that one of my most favorite
poets is Emily Dickinson. . . . "But never met this
fellow, / attended or alone, / without a tighter
breathing / and zero at the bone." She wrote short
poems, in clear different language. Not that they
are easy to understand, but they are easy to read. I

remember as a freshman that she was the only poet
I felt strongly about. I hated her. In the same class
I argued the worth of *Catcher in the Rye*. Now that
I've reversed my opinions, I wonder. Have I sold
out, grown up and gone to a white shirt/black tie
conformity? I guess not. But I'm watching myself
for further symptoms.

Of course Wallace Stevens was a vice-president
of Hartford Accident and Indemnity Company, and
that's similar to being an executive with Boeing.
And watch his poems disappear: "Chieftain Iffucan
of Azcan in Caftan / of tan with henna hackles,
halt!" Stevens I also fell strongly for and think he's
touched about as close as any to what I want when
I'm writing.

Kathy (she's not far away, ever, as her presence
means I can read and loaf and her absence means I
have to try to coordinate my hands and eyes, to
type) was gone today and will be gone again
tomorrow. So tomorrow I'll be banging the old
machine, not to write my diary but Army correspondence. Ugh!!

Time for bed.

30 August 1967, Wednesday Morning

It's 5:55 and I'm on my way to breakfast.

I'm back from breakfast and My Lan is playing
that old R&B recording of "Smoke Gets in Your
Eyes." " . . .Tears I cannot hide . . ."

"Never apologize, never explain."
—*Benjamin Jowett's advice to starting poets*

7:55 a.m.

Last night I went early to bed. I'm reading *Paterson* this morning at work as there is nothing much to do. I've read the thing, most of it, here and there in pieces and am now trying it front to back.

Today I get off at 4:00 to go eat dinner before guard duty, which starts at 6:00, and I get paid tomorrow morning and am off all day to sleep, although the sergeant major thinks he is going to limit us to four hours of compensatory time. But he's wrong, I hope. I'll be off all day tomorrow and then work on Friday, and then Saturday I leave on R&R and don't plan to be back at work 'til the Monday of the 11th. The sergeant major *could* have protected me from this unnecessary indignity of guard duty.

Things are so much the same these last few days that I have left here that there is not really much to say. It's rainy outside right now, and cloudy, and looks very Seattle-like. The rain is rattling against the window and I wish that I had fewer days left.

Monday when I begin work after R&R I'll have only 40 days and 40 nights, time enough for a Biblical John Huston type of flood (or other calamity), but most likely it won't happen, although it would make a nice ending to my Vietnam Journal.

Lt. Col. Rollins just said that SP5s are the backbone of the Army, and I said yes, the lower end.

Time for me to take a trip down the hall to the porcelain facilities (namely the shitter.) I'll soon be back.

I was right, here I am. Yesterday I spend the day reading Ed McBain novels, two of them. *Doll* and *Wedge of Something* or other. They move right along and the day goes quite swiftly. I've not yet had that trouble that I'm supposed to have—time slowing down. It still moves right on by. Maybe that last 40 days will drag, but I hope they won't.

Hong Kong beckons. That good food, that good room with bath, hot water and all the luxury. Those book shops, department stores, record stores. I'm all atremble with anticipation of it.

The elections are soon here. Saigon is off limits, but I'll be down there right in the middle of it all on the big day as I leave from Tan Son Nhut airport right down where old USARV used to be. It's been almost a year since I went through that airport coming into country. I remember the scene as well as if it were just 11 or 12 days ago rather than almost a full tour. The ceiling fans, the Vietnamese moving freight, the rats in the squalid latrine and the rows of bicycles under the sheds outside where we were loaded onto buses with steel grill wire on the windows. It'll be funny to ride again on buses that don't have that, and I'm sure I'll feel very vulnerable at first.

I got back my first roll of slides and not one of the roll came out. Better luck next time. The second roll won't come out either, for I opened the back of the camera when the roll wasn't rewound. What a dummy. Today I might be able to pick up a roll of black and white pictures that I took the last few weeks, last couple weeks actually. I know that they will come out fine, for I followed Dead Head Ed's instructions most of the time and was shooting pictures over his shoulder at subjects he had all warmed up by his personality. Things are much duller without Ed around.

I think I'll walk over to the paperback library and get something exciting (adventurous) to read.

12:10 p.m.

I guess I'll read some more of the book I checked out this morning from the library. It's called The Great Gatsby and is by Francis Scott Fitzgerald. It's one of the most poetic things I've read lately and reminds me often of the poetry of William Carlos Williams. "... It was deep summer on roadhouse roofs and in front of wayside garages, where new red gas-pumps sat out in pools of light ..." Fine stuff and very exciting the way the author just allows us glimpses of Gatsby in the first twenty pages, glimpses that raise a mystery and an interest in him.

He's just a theme evident so far, not a character, but it's fine stuff. Such a short novel I'll have no trouble finishing it in the next day at the most.

3:35 p.m.

I've been typing letters and endorsements most of the afternoon since last I typed on this entry. I've been humming a couple of songs all afternoon; songs will run through one's mind: Woody knows nothin' but pecking on a bough and Wanting you but still not having you, that soulful country-western classic.

Brian Epstein died. Rather unexpected to be just an ordinary, no-questions-asked death.

I leave in just a few minutes for bunker guard detail, which promises to be one more boondoggle as I'll have many hours tomorrow in which to read and relax.

31 August 1967, Thursday, 8:00 p.m.

I got paid today. I went in to get paid in the same uniform in which I stood guard—mud to my breast pockets, all mussed up, and walking like a zombie—reported to a new C.O., a lieutenant, and stumbled out. He asked his clerk if I was always like that and was properly reassured.

Last night we stumbled down a series of boards laid out across a beweeded rice paddy to our bunker for guard. The paddy filled with water during the night and emptied with the dawn tide's withdrawal. Ducks and frogs and earth moving machinery made noise all night, and I slept briefly on the floor wrapped in a poncho to protect myself from the trash. I was already wet to the skin from the afternoon rain. I thought about the sergeant major a time or two, while shivering awoke unkind thoughts.

This evening I feel great, my cold seems to be gone, and I enjoyed that day off today very much. This morning I showered, shaved, went to bed, and read *Billboard* 'til I went to sleep. I got up at 1:30, ate a sandwich at the club, picked up my laundry, and got thirty 4x5 pictures that I'd left for developing. I then went back to bed to read *The Great Gatsby* which I just finished. A fine poetic book. That surprised me a bit. But the biggest surprise was the grotesque humor with which the book is

filled. Things like: The eyes of doctor T.J. Eckle-
burg, which is a theme from the first to the last;
and the countless observations of the narrator, Nick
Carraway. A very fine book. As fresh as anything
I've ever read. "It has value only as a period piece
of the '20s." Most ridiculous comment I heard
somewhere. It approaches Dylan Thomas much of
the time in its descriptive prose. Not in the words
so much as the feeling of a dominant point of view,
a someone who looks and sees. "So when the blue
smoke of brittle leaves was in the air and the wind
blew the wet laundry stiff on the line I decided to
come back home." Or, " . . . what a grotesque thing a
rose is and how raw the sunlight was upon the
scarcely created grass." As Col. Ebby says, no
matter what it is he's just finished reading, with
the final slam of the thing to his desk, "Fine stuff."

Oh yes, on page 6, there begins a long bit
beginning "From East Egg, then, came the Chester
Beckers and the Leeches and a man named Bunsen,
whom I knew at Yale, and Doctor Webster Civet,
who was drowned last summer up in Maine." It
keeps going on and on. And it's so great and funny
—the names and the comments interlaced. Fine
stuff. How come nobody ever communicated to me
that I must read that book? It leaves Hemingway
looking shallow and outdated, at least in his novels.

Now I've got Patchen's book to read this evening, but I'm tired of reading. Oh well, I'm going to
read Patchen's book for a while now and listen to
the radio. I'll write more in the morning.

1 September 1967, Friday Morning

It's 5:40 and I didn't read any of Patchen's book but just listened to the radio and then went to sleep early. So today I'm very rested.

I go on R&R tomorrow. I report into Camp Alpha and sit around 'til my plane leaves for Hong Kong. I'm taking some books to read and hope I've time for them instead of details like picking up butts. Time to go eat breakfast.

2 September 1967, Saturday, 5:20 a.m.

Today is the day Charlie and I go down to Camp Alpha. Tomorrow we leave from there for Tan Son Nhut Airport, which is right next door, and then Hong Kong.

Last evening I packed a suitcase and tried to get everything together that I'll want with me in Hong Kong. Also I got my khakis ready to wear, with all the insignia, brass, etc. that has to be on the shirt.

Right now I'm listening to a big band program which seems to have replaced that folk music show that used to be on Saturday at this time. I don't care for the big band sound at all.

The lights just went on, so I'm going to shave now and continue this entry a little later.

6:20 a.m.

A friend (Rosie) just came by and told Clark and me that he got us a sedan for the day, so we won't have to take the bus down to Tan Son Nhut but will have first-class transportation. Rosie is a driver for our section and is going to Hawaii for R&R.

Also the supply room guy who is also leaving on R&R today just brought me a new pair of low quarters, still in the box. I would have had to borrow a pair if he hadn't gotten me a pair this morning, as I turned mine in. He leaves for Bangkok today.

Right now on the radio a man who is "a legend in his own time" is being interviewed—Captain Leonard Rodderick.

I'll be leaving here at about 2:30 this afternoon and 'til then I'm going to lounge around. First I'll shower.

9:00 p.m.

I'm at Camp Alpha at the Tan Son Nhut airport from which we leave tomorrow for Hong Kong, after our final briefing. Today we checked in at about 3:00 after shopping at the Tan Son Nhut PX where I bought three rolls of 36 black and white film. I'll preserve the experience on celluloid.

We rode down here in a sedan with the air conditioning broken, so it was a very stuffy ride. Saigon looked very different. It was siesta time, but the streets were especially deserted and traffic was the thinnest I've ever seen it. Tomorrow is election day and everybody is cautious of possible trouble. I wish I could have gotten out of the car and taken a roll of black and white film of the election posters which are stuck everywhere, but of course that would not have been wise.

When first we got here we got our initial briefing in a hot (stifling) little room, and filled out forms and were checked off on the flight manifest. I'm 54 and Charlie is 55, so we'll probably be sitting next to each other.

Today the PX had all kinds of records: blues, Junior Wells, Eric Burton, and tons of other good stuff. When first I got in country there was nothing like that.

This morning while sitting around the barracks killing time, waiting to leave, one of the guys from the orderly room came over and told me I had a call. I was naked, didn't want to move, and anyhow figured it was Sergeant Major Smith wanting to give me some sage advice, or worse. So I refused to go, "as I'm not properly attired." The crumb didn't know who it was. The orderly room is always like that. They expect blind obedience without giving any explanation. Well, I was in no mood to move.

In about ten seconds the runner was back, frothing at the mouth. "Top . . ." (first sergeant) " . . . says to get your ass over there, naked or not." So I ambled over in a pair of cutoffs. It was one of the lieutenant colonels from the office begging me to do a favor for him. Exchange a sweater for him in Hong Kong, and a couple of other things. Well, I'd rather not of course, but I said okay, if he'd bring the stuff to me, I'd be in the sack next door in my barracks.

He told me to be sure to explain to the first sergeant that he called me just to ask a personal favor, etc. I explained nothing to the first sergeant, just told him that the lieutenant colonel would be coming to see me and could he please be brought to my cubical. You've got to understand that an orderly room is run by a first lieutenant, and colonels scare the shit out of them. So the lieuten-

ant colonel came and they brought him to me, and
I'll exchange his moldy old sweater. This little story
is an example of the different role that rank plays
in company and section. The company (orderly
room) automatically assumes I'm being called for
disciplinary reasons (why else?). They think that
way.

I took a shower a few minutes ago and the
water, although unheated, was about 50 degrees
warmer than the ice water in our showers up at
Long Binh. It felt great.

Oh yes, today Charlie got his ETS orders, so I
should be getting mine pretty soon. He leaves five
days after I do, but he's further up in the alphabet.
Those orders surely look good. Fine Army.

3 September 1967, Sunday, 3:30 p.m.

Well, I'm really up in the air right now. About
midway in flight between Saigon and Hong Kong. I
just ate and it was an okay meal, nothing exotic.
The beans were bright green and cold, and like
plastic. The meat was fine.

I have *Memoirs of a Shy Pornographer* on my
lap and an Air Force major sitting next to me.
Charlie is somewhere in the front; I'm way in the
back, the last passenger to board the plane. Charlie
and I plan to stay at the Hilton. When we get off
the plane we'll make final plans. It's about $10 per
night for a single room, which is reasonable. The
cheapest hotel is $4, but there is no reason to
scrimp. The Hilton has a swimming pool, restaur-
ants and all that old stuff.

All morning at Camp Alpha was spent in paperwork and processing—countless hot, stuffy rooms, much paperwork, and no pen or pencil provided, so I used the same dull #3 pencil with which I'm writing this entry.

The flight so far has been very smooth and I've slept much of the time. Travel has always acted as a soporific to me.

The stewardesses are bustling about, three of them: One old one, one skinny, boney one, and one big broad-assed one who keeps boredly flipping her hair back with a quick twist of her head. Annoying, but then I don't have to look at her, do I?

They handed out magazines earlier when I was asleep, and I've now gotten hold of the *Life* magazine and will devour it.

4 September 1967, Monday, 11:00 a.m.

We arrived in glorious Hong Kong last evening, had our briefing (avoid guides, etc.) and were released on our own. Charlie and I are staying at the International Hotel, Kowloon. We've had a very fine time so far. Encountered no trouble, no curfew, no food shortage, plenty of hot water, and friendly people. Last night we went to a few bars. Today we had parfaits at Lindy's Delicatessen, banana splits at the Dairy Farm. Last night Charlie and I and another guy here from Saigon, Roy, had a ten course Chinese meal. Not one dish was identifiable to me, but all was delicious.

Today we went to the China Fleet Club (a PX) and bought some stuff. I got two pairs of socks, a camera tripod, a pair of desert boots, a foulard shirt. We used taxis to go everywhere, about $1 to

$1.50 Hong Kong Dollars for each ride (that's about 17 to 28 cents American) We rode the Star Ferry several dozen times today back and forth from Hong Kong to Kowloon.

Oh yes, we decided to stay at this hotel so we'd have more money to buy things with. A good reason, I think. The hotel is very nice, air conditioned, centrally located, and all that. I'm listening to the radio right now. Weird stuff they play. Just heard a story by Ambrose Bierce, "Late One Night."

Today we went up the Peak Tram to Victoria Peak, 1,809 feet above sea level, the guide book says. We took slides and ate Nutty Buddy ice cream cones.

This city is a great contrast to Saigon. A clean, western city. Huge department stores. Stylish women, all miniskirt clad, and all about their own business or with men. This city isn't the open air whore house Saigon has become. Oh, there are women around, and guys who whisper "GI want feelthy pictures?", but mostly they are trying to sell custom made shirts and all that.

This city seems to have many young married couples (in their twenties) with very small children in tow (American tourists, I mean). When Charlie and I walk down the streets, the touts thrust cards into our hands.

From Victoria Peak it was evident that this city is carved into stone. Huge buildings sitting on the cliffs, and green all around. Like the "I Spy" episodes shot here.

There are things that tickle me about the place. Most personal are the signs "Do Not Spit, $500 fine" posted everywhere. I mean what an inhibitor! To have fun and not spit—and all the signs. "Beware

Pickpockets." The signs here are quite literate of
course, a contrast to the ludicrous attempts in
Saigon.

Tomorrow we'll again ride the ferry; finish up
Charlie's fitting for a Hong Kong suit; Take the
Kowloon night tour; Chinese dinner, opera, and all
that jazz.

I'm using this seven days to grow a moustache.
Should be quite unambiguously revolting by Monday. And Col. Ebby will have just left on R&R and
by the time he gets back it will be luxuriantly black
and spiky. (I may sicken of it, and off it will fall.)

Some bargaining here is done. Tonight Charlie,
Roy, and I pretended we were interested in old
ivory snuff boxes and hit every ivory shop for blocks
around. They must still wonder what hit them.
They have these boxes and bottles resembling tor-
toises, fruits, seeds, nuts, animals, little old men,
all kinds of crazy things. We bought none. But Roy
bought an opium pipe for $28 Hong Kong, about $3
American. Old ivory with a pewter bowl.

Don and Phil Everly are singing "A Legend in
My Time," a fine sad song.

Back to snuff boxes, I saw two that I think I'll
buy tomorrow, in the shape of cockroaches,
grotesque and very unusual.

Pat Boone just limped through a song, "I'll Find
You."

I bought a book today to read myself to sleep
with—John D. MacDonald's *Bright Orange for the
Shroud* — for when I'm away from the lulling
(stupefying) routine of the Army. I find it hard to
relax and sleep.

I guess I'll read now. And then, perhaps, to
sleep.

5 September 1967, Tuesday, 3:30 p.m.

Today Charlie pounded on my door at 8:00, woke me up, and we went to Lindy's East with Roy and had lox, bagels, cream cheese, and San Miguel beer for breakfast. We then went to the PX where I bought a sheepskin coat, which I've always coveted, and had it boxed and shipped. It's quite a coat, like the ones Glenn Ford, Jimmy Stewart, and the boys wear in the cowboy flicks.

For lunch we ate at the Dairy Farm. I had a thick chocolate milk shake and an open chicken sandwich thing, which had a very fancy name but was still very good.

I've thought more about my python boots and decided how to salvage them so I can wear them in spite of the smallness of the left boot. I'll have them re-soled and re-heeled and re-fitted to my foot by a Seattle cobbler when I get home. That shouldn't cost more than ten or fifteen dollars, I would think.

Here, every woman under thirty-five wears her skirt way above the knees. Very nice. The dresses here most popular are like mini mini minis, very bright and short.

I think I'll go down to the street and dicker about those snuff boxes. I'll write more in a bit.

6:15 p.m.

I bought the snuff boxes and then Roy and I (Charlie had a tummy ache and was resting) went through an million shirting shops and drove 'em crazy with requests. Like orange paisley overprinted with brown stripes, green paisley underprinted with black, etc. We found a place that had the above.

Last night when I looked at the two roach snuff boxes, they asked $25 for the larger and $20 for the smaller, or $45. Today, she started at $40 for both and I started at $30. I ended up paying $32 after starting out of the shop four or five times. I paid, in American dollars, $5.50 for both.

We also found a fine British book store. I bought four novels by Georges Simenon — *Pedigree, The Widower, The Fate of the Malous,* and *Maigret Takes a Room* — about 50 or 60 cents each. Hard to get in the States. *Pedigree* is his very long autobiographical novel, the Maigret is one of his famous detective series, and the other two are his short ones written in a week or so.

Tonight I believe we'll go on the Kowloon night tour and perhaps tomorrow we'll hit the dairy farms or the fishing village, or both.

A note on the weather. It's been sort of Seattle summerish, with rain now and again. Very pleasant actually.

They have a bill here that's worth $500 Hong Kong, or about $87.40 American, that's about as big as a window-shade. Folded up, it's more cumbersome than a map of Wyoming. They don't last long, of course.

I ran out of paper. It's 6:30 and I guess we'll start getting ready for the evening tour.

> *I wish I were close*
> *To you as the wet skirt of*
> *A salt girl to her body.*
> *I think of you always.*
> *— Akahito*

6 September 1967, Wednesday, 6:35 p.m.

Today was a rainy day and I bought an umbrella. Remembrance of Seattle. I felt as though I were carrying a sword. Today I hit three or four book shops, bought some Simenon books and two volumes of verse: *The Penguin Book of Modern Verse* translation and *Penguin Modern Poets:* Levertov, Rexroth, and W.C. Williams, fine poets all.

For breakfast today I had a cheeseburger, very novel and not recognizable as such, almost Chinese in flavor. The bun was on both sides covered with concentric circles, as if baked in a mold. For lunch I had a pastrami sandwich, San Miguel beer, and cheesecake at Lindy's East.

Today I decided that I'm going to have one of the ivory roaches mounted with an eye so I can wear it on a chain as an amulet. I was fitted for two shirts today in the shop where Roger Smith gets his shirts (big deal). Very unusual shirts—paisleys, one green, one blue, overprinted with stripes.

The Simenon books I bought are *The Mouse, Account Unsettled, Ticket of Leave, In Case of Emergency, Black Rain, Act of Passion, The Premier Sunday, The Hatter's Ghosts,* and *Stain on the Snow.*

Also today I went with Charlie and Roy to their final fittings—suits, sports coats, shirts, whatever they were having made. Tomorrow I must shop for the list from the lieutenant colonel. I must.

Tonight we plan to ride the Peak Tram and see the city from the peak at night. Tomorrow we will go to the Tiger Balm Garden.

Tonight we also shall revisit the place we ended up last night, the Fire Cracker Lounge in the President Hotel. They have an all girl band there (sisters 14 to 20 years old) who are fantastic.

Their youth, their sweet and absolutely uncoy delivery, their interaction on the stage, and their great use of guitar, drums, and organ make them closer to a religious experience than any rock and roll band I've ever heard. They sang and played all kinds of songs—Motown, Supremes, Nancy Sinatra, Stones. But they ended with a "Sugar Pie Honey Bunch," which lasted almost half an hour, that dwarfed the Four Tops. It showed the girls moving with their voices and instruments to weave separate tapestries of sound. And as they went their separate ways, they joined up perfectly in a supplication and a praise in the fine chorus, "Sugar Pie Honey . . ."

Before we went to the Fire Cracker, we ranged up and down the whole Suzie Wong area, handing out to the hawkers and shills the cards they'd given us the night before. A bar girl named Rose, as an attempt to get us into her bar (girls stand in front of the girl bars, extending their hospitality) jumped on Roy's back. He grabbed her legs, hitched her up pig-a-back and gave her a ride for about three blocks. All the hawkers, street walkers, barrel calkers, and miscellaneous apple knockers stood flabbergasted and then laughed mightily. Rose (a very happy girl unlike Saigon bar girls) enjoyed it immensely and protested only tokenly. Great fun, and not costing one cent.

We ate dinner at a Russian restaurant over a bakery (it was Russian too). I had piroshky, borscht, beef stroganoff. The food was glorious, cheap, fine. I couldn't half finish my stroganoff. Also throughout the meal a baker kept strolling through the room with trays of a variety of dinner rolls, just baked, hot from the oven. My check came to about $2 American. I was so full I thought I'd die.

Last night after we left the Fire Cracker we returned to our hotel on foot. Stepped over people asleep on the covered sidewalks and in general kept looking over our shoulders.

I've saving all newspapers, one from each day of my stay here, as a primer for my memory when I attempt to remember these few days here. This time here in Hong Kong has released me from the dulling safety of Army ritual, a safety from the extremes of anticipation of the end of it—and the beginning of something new.

My moustache is quite revolting, black and spiky, and my hair is shaggy. But still I can be spotted as a GI a block away because of my short sideburns and the short hair on the back of my head and neck.

Right now the radio announcer is narrating a funeral of two political characters. I've not read today's paper yet but I vaguely remember death by assassination.

The radio announcer just said we're returning to 24-hour water availability, and now the government spokesman is berating the newspapers for a premature announcement of same and "teaching us our business."

It's time now for me to venture forth for the evening. I'll write more tomorrow.

7 September 1967, Thursday, 7:20 p.m.

Here it is my last evening in glorious Hong Kong. Tonight we plan to go to the Fire Cracker Room again and perhaps go up the Peak Tram.

Last night we hit the Fire Cracker Room late, sat there at a fine table for two and a half hours and were never asked to buy a drink. No cover charge, and the entertainment is great, and the people who dance are fun to watch. Earlier last evening we sat in a luxurious place on the top floor of he Miramar Hotel (The Purple Room) and drank for hours looking at a view of the city and the harbor similar to that from the Space Needle. That cost next to nothing. We had dish after dish of free nuts and other crunchies, fine service, and also live entertainment.

Today early I got up and got the lieutenant colonel's shopping finished. Pain in the ass dealing with Indian shop keepers to exchange a beaded sweater. Also I had to argue a Seiko watch from $21 (U.S.) to $10 (U.S.) I only got it down to $12 (U.S.) And the radio tubes !! Had to be ordered from the warehouse. I got them. Huge things.

Then Charlie, Roy, and I travelled all over the city taking pictures, and looking at motorcycles. After that we ate fried rice and went to Tiger Balm Garden. A cruddy place filled with beggars and guys selling dirty slides. But from there is a beautiful view of the tin can slums covering the green, terraced hillsides. Green, lush, hundreds of steps leading up into the dwellings.

After that we rented a cab and went to Repulse Bay. I remember the Cary Grant / Alfred Hitchcock movie (I think) about the cat burglar (also Grace

Kelly). Well, that was filmed on the Riviera, and this today rivaled that in every way. No people at all. We saw two soldiers and flattered them into allowing their bikinied girl friends into posing with us in some beach pictures. The beach is clean, white, the water warm, hotels right on the beach. The taxi ride round trip was on a twisty scenic road, high above the beaches and through magnificent villas.

Tonight earlier I picked up my two tailored shirts, and they are perfect in fit and sartorially without blemish. All I've eaten since lunch is a rum and cola and some mango ice cream, so I believe I'll go to dinner now and then finish up the evening. I still have to pack, or rather shoe-horn all the stuff into my suitcase, and prepare my uniform. But that shouldn't take long. This will be the last entry in Hong Kong, and the next will of course be from Vietnam. I guess I won't work on Friday. Maybe Saturday and then I'm off Sunday, a day of rest. But I'm well rested now, having not forgotten to sleep each night. I've slept well and heavily after getting accustomed to the change.

Homeward Bound!
I wish I was
Homeward Bound!
    —Simon & Garfunkle

8 September 1967, Friday, 5:45 p.m.

Simon and Garfunkle are now singing "Homeward Bound" and I feel short. I'm back in Vietnam, sitting on my bunk, looking at all my stuff I got in

Hong Kong, and thinking about coping with Sergeant Major Smith and his ghoulish games again.

Last night I ate dinner, walked around 'til about 11:00 looking at the sights, and then went to my room to finish my packing and read *Account Unsettled* by Simenon. Got up this morning at 6:30. Went to the airport, flew up and away. On the flight I read *The Mouse* by Simenon. Fine books. Short, introspective characterization, good plot and detail, detail, detail.

When we went into the orderly room to sign in, our C.O. asked us a million questions about Hong Kong, as he plans to meet his wife there. We gave him the scoop and will give him a bunch of brochures and booklets. Then I dropped off my laundry and film to be developed.

7:55 p.m.

Just now I was reading the first few pages of G. Simenon's *The Widower,* and an instrumental version of the Everely Brothers' old hit "If Ever I Want You, all I have to do is dream, dream, dream..." came on. A beautiful song and one of my favorites. And it reminded me that this morning when I was awakened by the phone in my hotel room I was dreaming of My Darling. Rarely do I remember my dreams, but when they are interrupted and I'm suddenly awakened, I'm more likely to. I was dreaming very definitely of my Jungle Princess, for all the good dreams ever do. She's gone. In fact, she was never really there, and I must face the rest of my life and learn to take charge, to not be merely a chip on a wave.

9 September 1967, Saturday Morning

It's 5:45. The Guy Lombardo band is doing
"Cuddle Up a Little Closer." Nauseating stuff. I
don't know who wants to listen to that old junk.
Somebody plays it though, so there must be a
demand.

I've found out that I work all day today and
tomorrow too, so I've a big week ahead of me. Right
now I'm bound for a good old Army breakfast.

3:00 p.m.

I have received a copy of my separation orders.
It's all in code so I don't understand all of it, but
it's just what I wanted, and everything thus far is
going smoothly. Lt. Col. Rollins assures me nothing
will happen to keep me from getting out of the
Army on 22 October 1967. Good news, eh? I'm glad
to get them as I can now start sending home hold
baggage free. Next weekend I hope to start on this.

Today has been a very busy day, at least since
12:30. This morning Lt. Col. Rollins and I talked
most of the time. Col. Ebby left on his R&R late
this morning, and before he left he suggested I get
rid of the moustache. I don't like it much but think
I'll keep it for another week anyhow to see how the
thing is shaping up.

This afternoon I've been getting my filing and
suspense in shape, but Lt. Col. Rollins took care of
most of it while I was gone, so it's now in good
shape. If the WAC had been doing it, I'd never have
gotten it straightened out. She's gone on R&R, too.

Today I got another box of slides. Of the roll of
20 slides I took with my new camera, only 10 of

them came out, but I hope to do better on the ones I took on R&R. I'll know on 11 September when I get them back. I really hope most of them come out. The ones that did come out this time were so much clearer and full of detail compared to those taken with my cheap box camera. I wonder if Sergeant Major Smith is behind this. Could the tentacles of the khaki mafia reach into the recesses of gook film processing? Why not? I must not give in to my paranoiac tendencies.

Some random notes:

Kathy qualifies only technically as a woman. She has abdicated the role of woman and become a soldier, and a sorry one at that.

I don't get along with Major Tief, although we have a truce lately. Right now he is in the hospital for a bad leg. I hope he improves, but slowly, like about 42 days. With him gone, my only adversary is Sergeant Major Smith.

I've not drunk much since I came to Vietnam. In Hong Kong I had about three drinks, not together.

A colonel just stuck his head through my door here and said: You know the old saying about cultivation of your upper lip. I said no sir. He retorted: Why cultivate on your upper lip something that grows wild around your asshole? A good folk saying, I think.

I haven't been high since I got over here, and on purpose because it would just intensify my loneliness and cut through the shield that I've built around myself as protection from dwelling on the fact that I'm so cut off from what I want!

Ed is gone, ETS'd, and now a civilian. Today Charlie got a letter from him that I've yet to read. I

must go burn the trash and then will complete this
entry.

Later:

Just got back from burning the trash. It's 5:05
and only twenty-five more minutes and I'll be off
duty 'til 7:30 tomorrow morning.

Last night the chaplain's assistants were having
a beer blast as one of them is so short he'll be
leaving in a couple of days. I went up there and was
drinking beer with them and thought of some of the
slides I bought in Hong Kong which were really
rank. So ugly that they aren't even pornography.
About five of them are normal playboy type cheesecake shots. The other fifteen show a girl with her
old pins spread a mile and a cunt the size of the
Grand Canyon, and the color of fresh catsup. The
first few slides got a good response, but when one of
the really awful ones was popped on the screen
after a few normal ones, they were almost stunned.
And then the cat-calls began. Shown that way they
were really funny, but how awful they are. Just
shot after shot of an ugly oriental girl spread out on
a bed with a fan over her face and her legs spread.
Graceless and lacking in any sexual invitation.

I've been thinking about something somebody
said to me in a letter. No, I guess it's not selling
out to change one's opinions. But an amazing
number of my beliefs have held up well over the
years, and I expect they will continue to. Even after
all of this.

Time to go eat and then I'll spend the evening
reading Simenon. It's now after 5:30, so I'm off to

dinner and the billets and I'll finish this later tonight.

Later Still:

It's 8:55 and Roy Acuff is playing a sentimental harmonica piece on the Opry, and I'm lonesome.

We got a letter from Dead Head Ed today which explained all the procedures we'll go through at Oakland. It'll take about twenty-four hours, maybe a bit less. They cut orders there for home-issue light weight green woolies and sew on all the insignia, patches, etc. The green thing is what I wear on the plane home.

"Build me a cabin in the corner of glory land," the radio just said.

"Gunsmoke" just came on the radio, yes, the radio. Shades of old L&M cigarette commercials.

I read, or rather finished reading Simenon's *The Widower*. Another fine short novel. I don't understand his novels very well, but of course I don't let that hamper my enjoyment.

I'm going to bed now and most likely to sleep.

10 September 1967, Sunday Morning

It's 6:30 and Charlie is cursing because he can't find his blousing rubbers. We both work today and I plan to do very little except putter around with my paperwork. So I'm on my way to breakfast. And then to the office.

> *"In my novel, everything is true while nothing is accurate."*
>
> —*G. Simenon, in Preface to Pedigree*

When I write my Vietnam War novel I intend to keep the above dictum in mind.

7:45 p.m.

This will be a short entry, as I'm very tired. Today I worked at my desk 'til about 3:00 and from then on I read *Black Rain* by G. Simenon. I've read most of it. It's a lot like Celine—third person—fine stuff.

I'm now off to sleep. I'll write more in the morning.

11 September 1967, Monday, 5:55 a.m.

It's morning. Not only did I go to sleep last night at 8:00, but I over-slept this morning too.

It's now 6:20, and I've eaten, if you want to call it that. "Love Me Tender" just played on the radio. That brings back the past.

Today is going to be a big day, as no WAC will be there to type, nor for the rest of the week either. So I'll have to actually do the work myself. And with that big bird, Sergeant Major Smith, looking over my shoulder.

This morning I'm going to work early and read *Black Rain* 'til 7:30.

12 September 1967, Tuesday, 7:35 p.m.

For one reason or another I didn't write anything more yesterday, mostly because I've not done

anything to write about and I'm so short I've
written myself out.

Today was a bummer day. I typed all day
lickety-split with hardly time to catch my breath.
I've got some stuff left over for tomorrow, but as I
go in early (at 6:00) to open up, make coffee, etc., I
guess I'll be even by 7:30 a.m.

Today a bug fell out of my desk, and in my
eagerness to smash him with my waste can, I
smashed my thumb instead. It bled profusely (as
they say), but a small bandaid stanched it.

It's raining outside with a sound like a freight
train roaring past. Rain particles are coming
through the screen of course.

I got my slides back. They all came out. One
thing I didn't do is follow Dead Head Ed's one Royal
Rule of Pitcher Taking— "Get fuckin' close to the
subject!" I've got lots of fine distance shots but few
closeups. This Sunday Charlie and I plan to go to
Binh Hoa and take a few pictures. I plan to take 15
slides and 36 black and white—closeups—everyone
a face, or still lifes of objects.

13 September 1967, Wednesday Morning

I guess I don't open up today, although I thought
I was supposed to. So here I am at 5:35, ready to go
eat. And I'm listening to the Statler Brothers sing
"I Still Miss Someone." My stomach is all cramped
from hunger, not to be appeased by the slop I'll soon
be swilling at the mess hall. But I can wait 38 days
'til strawberries and cream everyday and dancing in
the streets.

5:35 p.m.

I've not listened to "Ode to Billy Joe" again. I've not had a record player readily available, nor the time I used to have. Here it is really mostly work and little play. Even though during the day I have plenty of time to sit around, I'm tied to the office and I'm not supposed to write letters, read, etc. But of course nobody would say anything about it to me. I'm too short for them to really touch me.

Today Major Tief got back from the hospital with a nasty limp and a chip on his shoulder about how badly our boys are being treated in the hospital: dirty sheets, substandard service, etc. His heart's in the right place, but then he jumped me about long hair, moustache, etc. I gave him hell right back. All in a jocular manner of course. He left after being in the office for two hours. Lt. Col. Rollins left early today also and put me in charge of covering for him, so here I am.

Only three more days this week without the valuable assistance of old Fat Kath. Also when Col. Ebby returns from R&R I think that Don, my replacement, will be moving into the room so I'll not have much to do except mark time 'til I'm gone. I hope I'll be able to easily readjust to being with real round-eyed women. When a girl enters the room, I feel like John Wayne looks in one of his "Oh Gosh, Ma'am" roles, in which he drops his hat in the punch bowl and steps in the pastry.

I guess I'll go relieve my bowels, then return and read some more of *The Survivors* by G. Simenon.

14 September 1967, Thursday Morning

It's 5:35 a.m. and I'm listening to Johnny Paycheck sing "Orange Blossom Special." "... I'm goin' down to Florida, get some sand in my shoes...." Good idea.

Last night I read, or finished, *The Survivors,* and at 10:00 went to sleep. Next I'm going to read *Maigret Takes a Room* for a change of pace. A mystery novel.

Time to go eat.

12:45 p.m.

Good old Slim Harpo is on the radio. "Baby, Scratch My Back" actually made a rating as one of the top 50 singles of 1966. And it's real blues.

I'm looking forward to being cold again after a year of being cold only at night. It will be nice to put on boots and wool socks and a heavy sheepskin coat and maybe even a hat and still feel the cold. It will be a real treat.

Things are stacking up in Lt. Col. Rollins' in basket. We've gotten some priority junk in so all the other stuff is just sitting, and it's building up in a huge heap. If he gets to the point this afternoon where he can attack the stuff, I'll have a very busy day the rest of the day. Up 'til now I've done nothing except read and finish Simenon's book, *Maigret Takes a Room.*

I guess I'll now go and look for a thing that I can't find that goes with another thing that came in the mail today. I'll be in mild trouble if I can't find it, but I'm too short to really give a shit. Even

Sergeant Major Smith (that malignant carbuncle on the face of the U.S. Army) would be challenged to change my attitude.

I did shave off my moustache this morning. My upper lip feels better, but it looks naked.

Later:

It's been a busy day since I last wrote. I've run a few errands and picked up the mail. This footwork emphasized to me the importance of arch supports that I've not had since I returned from R&R. While I was gone they disappeared somewhere. I imagine the mamasan got them and is using them for soup stock or somesuch, but my feet and knees are hurting me the same as in basic, so I'm going to have to do something about it, I guess.

Sunday I won't be going to Bien Hoa to take pictures as nobody is available to go with me and it's not wise to go there alone. I'm not going to waste the rolls of film here in the area for there is nothing here to take pictures of. So Sunday I'll most likely just sit around and rest and read and write letters, which activity is probably best anyhow. I've got plenty of reading material of all types and for most moods.

I think Lt. Col. Rollins expects me to stay here this evening to type a big emergency thing for him, and I suppose I shall. Actually it's 5:45 and I'm due to leave here in only 45 minutes, but I guess it'll be later than that.

I'm getting quite irritated at having to do all this work myself and look forward to Fatty (Kathy) being back to fumble through again on it in her inimitable fashion. She thinks that she'll not have to work 'til Monday, but Sergeant Major Smith scheduled her for Sunday, the same as he did Charlie and me when we returned on Saturday last. Maybe she's been uncooperative. One of the clerks will leave for the U.S. on Wednesday, and they have him scheduled to work on Sunday, but I guess he'll talk his way out of it.

I'll write more later tonight as I've got some stuff to do now.

9:10 p.m.

I'm showered and ready for bed. I just saw two pictures Charlie took of me in Hong Kong. My moustache is barely noticeable. I'm going to bed now. I'm tired as I worked 'til 8:00 tonight and must be at work tomorrow to open up at 6:00.

16 September 1967, Saturday, 6:55 p.m.

I didn't write yesterday, but here I am again today.

I can't phone anyone at home from here as there aren't any facilities here for that purpose, and Saigon is off limits. I could have phoned from Hong Kong easily, but didn't want to spend the money on something that would upset me more than it would please me.

I've all day tomorrow off. I plan to stay right here and read and relax and watch TV. They have a program on experimental films. Sounded interesting.

I went downtown Bien Hoa with Michael this afternoon and took pictures of the local nationals.

I'm still interested in the country, but I'm eager to leave. I don't have any definite plans, but I want to get home and start working on them anyway. Just to get back after all this long time. . . .

Well I guess I'll read some George Simenon. I'm going to sleep in tomorrow.

17 September 1967, Sunday, 7:15 p.m

I've spent the entire day in bed reading, except for meals and attending cursorily to my toilet. I've yet to shave or shower today. I've been reading Simenon all day. I finished *The Stain on the Snow* this morning, and today read *The Fate of the Malous* and *Act of Passion*. A quote from the latter: "It is terrifying to think that we are all human beings, all of us forced to bend our backs, more or less, under an unknown sky, and that we refuse to make the least little effort to understand one another."

I wonder why that is, why do we do that way. I see a typical example of the above every day in my own dismissal of Kathy as a WAC, and Major Tief as a drunk, and even Sergeant Major Smith. Maybe it's an attempt on my part to shield all human vulnerability of mine. Or just an innate viciousness, but its something to be resisted, of that I'm sure. Simenon comes closer to recording human experience in its stifling reality than any other writer I can think of, except perhaps Celine.

It's raining now, there are cigarette butts on the floor around a crumpled Pall Mall package, and lightning is crackling in static on the church music droning on the radio—and I'm lonely and want someone.

21 September 1967, Thursday, 9:10 a.m.

I got candy from someone back home yesterday and appreciate it very much. We shared one of the pecan rolls here in the office and I ate one Mountain Bar. I'm hoarding the rest as the ants don't seem to be as sharp up here as they were at Tan Son Nhut.

I had a very good time in Hong Kong. It's quite a place, and I'm glad we were not intimidated by the inflammatory headlines into going elsewhere as we didn't run into any trouble of any kind. I read a few days ago that a barracks was bombed (I forget the name) in Kowloon. We walked by that barracks several times late at night on our way to our hotel, as it was quite close to our hotel. But it's just like the newspapers and Saigon. We'd spend a quiet day downtown, and upon reading the newspapers the next day we'd think we must have been in a different town by the descriptions of the things that allegedly took place.

I took 136+ slides and they all came out fine, although the mounting is less than perfect. I had them developed here on post and they don't do as well as they might.

When I get home I'll have to go golfing at least once so I can say I did. I guess it's a harmlessly strenuous form of exercise, although in principle I'm opposed to all forms of exercise, harmless or otherwise.

I read the other day that Seattle had a 95-degree high and a 57-degree low, which I think rather peculiar for this time of the year. If it lasts another month, I'll have little adapting to do from the weather here. We don't have forest fires here of course, except for the ones that we deliberately set to kill the locals, burn their homes and their crops.

I'm looking forward to seeing my old friend Randy again. I'm sure he's not changed over much in the last year or two. Most people don't. I'm told by some that everybody will have changed and all my old friends and buddies will have nothing in common with me any more now that I've been in the Army, but the Army got hold of me too late to change me very much. As they are painfully aware most of the time.

Yesterday all the clerks in my section who were not yet SP5 made it, so now we have the only section in the command in which every clerk is at least a SP5. The only reason we all made it was that we used every method, licit and illicit, to force the section to promote us. The officers of course were for the promotions, but the NCOs took fifteen years to make their E-5 back in "aught-8" so they wish to prevent anybody else, especially US, from making it any earlier. We won that battle, just as we eventually win all of them. The old saying about the greasy wheel getting the squeak or whatever is a true one. Of course my old nemesis Sergeant Major Smith might have something to say about that. I'll have to keep an even closer eye on him, I guess.

I look forward very much to getting back home so I can discuss all of this with real people and not have to rely on these entries, which are harder and harder for me to write the shorter I get, as you can tell by the length of time between some of them

these days. I've still got the time to write, but the
motivation is fast dissipating.

The office that I work in continues to be a
congenial one. Col. Ebby just came back from R&R
to Hawaii, Kathy just returned from R&R in Penang, and Lt. Col. Rollins is so short that he's always
in a good mood (he retires in fifty days after
twenty-five years in the Army). So therefore it
should be no great strain on me to finish up the
next thirty or so days which I have left before I
depart forever these shores in this embattled land.

Time to put my fingers to the typewriter in
official business.

25 September 1967, Monday, 7:15 a.m.

I finished off the last Mountain Bar day before
yesterday. Soon the Army will be handing me the
final money that I'll get from them. And in a couple
of days will be my last regular Army pay day.
Another landmark passed.

I hope the good Seattle weather lasts a bit
longer, but if there were snow on the ground when
I arrived I'd adjust rapidly. I hope my sheepskin
coat arrives before I do, in case I need the protection of it against any temperature below 65 degrees.

Many servicemen go to Hawaii on their way
home, but I see no reason for that. It's no good
unless you can meet a wife or lover there, and I
lack both right now. Other than that, the place
would hold no more magic than Dubuque, and that's
a dull place, I'm sure.

I'm sure I'll want to dig out my old Underwood
when I return home, as there will be a few things

I'll want to type. I know that a keyboard on a portable would seem minute to hands used to typing on an Adler with an acre of keys and type twice as big as normal.

It will be fun being a civilian again, but I'm sure the readjustment won't be entirely painless as any reentry to the U.S. after any absence of more than a year is a shocking one, the anthropologists always assured me (and I've been gone much longer.) I've girded my loins for the anomie that they tell me I'll feel, so I guess I'll make it.

Yes, it's the 22nd of October that I'll be leaving Vietnam. (That doesn't leave me much time to talk my boss into letting me take that helicopter ride I've been nagging him about.) It will take about twenty-four hours, my recently processed buddies write me, to be ground through the out-processing mill at Oakland. That time is jammed with junk to do, but I'm sure I'll be so excited that I'll hardly be able to sign my name.

I guess I'll type some letters, or at least attempt it before I start getting work to do.

27 Sept. 1967, Wednesday, 8:50 p.m.

Percy Sledge is singing "Love Me Tender" and a strong nostalgia (combined with a malaise) is of course gripping me as it does much of the time these last days in Vietnam.

I went on guard last night at 6:00 and guarded the bunker last night, for I hope the last time, 'til this morning at 6:00. I returned to the barracks this morning, and read L'Amour's *The Sky-Liners,* a further episode in the continuing saga of the Sack-

ett Clan. A fine book, funny and ethnic. Then I
slept 'til noon and went to work this afternoon, not
really doing anything much except burning garbage
at 4:00, a detail I'll be glad to never see again. But
which I'll be performing every other night 'til I
depart this fair land, thanks to a certain sergeant
major. Soon I'll be beyond the reach of his bloody
talons.

The days are hot lately, little rain, and the red
clay is not allowing the painstakingly-sowed grass
to come up, a fact that bothers me not a bit.

Tomorrow I'll probably get my port call; it will
have to be for 22 October as anything earlier would
foul up my ETS.

I still haven't heard whether or not my sheepskin coat arrived, as I sent it to an old address. I'm
rather fatalistic in my belief that as I didn't know
the new address, the coat will wander like Halley's
Comet through the ether, never to be caught hold of
again. I hope I'm wrong.

I guess I'll read *Tender is the Night* for a while
'til I fall asleep. The Four Tops just came on: "It's
the same old song, but with a different meaning
since you've been gone..." Enough to bring an
almost blubber, or a bit of a sob to me, with a
feeling of loss. Then Bobby Gentry came on with
her ode, which she now sings. . . .

28 September 1967, Thursday, 12:40 p.m.

I've got Sunday duty again and have another CQ
duty coming up. I hope that maybe I'll have time
Saturday to go into Bien Hoa and take a few more
black and white pictures, but I might not have the

energy. Not that I'm working hard, I'm not. But I feel enervated and lack any real spirit to do anything. I am almost overcome by a malaise; paralyzed really.

The weather here continues to be hot and I've got about six different kinds of body rash, most of which will disappear when I leave, I hope.

Today I cleaned out my desk of all my clutter and boxed up everything that I want to keep and then threw away the rest. I guess I'll read more in *Tender is the Night* for a while.

10:00 p.m.

Tonight I polished up my python boots and they are truly outstanding, that's all. I've got Sunday duty this week. I hope that I'll have time to do nothing. The same thing I do all week. Today all I did all day long was read *Tender is the Night* and type a letter for W.C. Westmoreland's signature. Kathy worked on it all yester afternoon and most of the morning but couldn't do it. I typed it letter perfect in an hour with my index fingers. Hooray for me. Kathy has willingly done all my work for me lately. I'm so short I'm a prima donna and the people I work directly with (Kathy, Lt. Col. Rollins, Col. Ebby) try to protect me from all hostile pressures, including Sergeant Major Smith.

Tonight I've been reading the September *Esquire*. I'll soon be among the living again. I'll have my total liberation from these countless months of formational life. I think the cool air of Seattle will clean up the sixty kinds of scrofula I've proliferating in tiny patches in the various corners of my epidermis—I hope.

29 September 1967, Friday, 8:00 p.m.

Another day gone. I'm still reading *Tender is the Night*. That book is permeated with a perverted sexuality, an unseen but suspected presence only hinted at. The following questions are in my mind:

1. What did Mr. McKisco see in the bathroom that caused her to say, "Well, upstairs I came upon a scene, my dears . . ."
2. What was that damn duel really about?
3. Why wasn't Dick Diver practicing medicine?

Fitzgerald's books have much gothic mystery about them, almost a Henry Jamesian circumlocution. But this book also has some sloppy writing in it. I can see where he could begin revising. But even so it's one of the best books on marriage I've read. He gets at a lot of stuff other writers are too masculine to see, or too insensitive. He also has some funny lists in this book, as in *Gatsby*.

Here's another quote from *Tender is the Night*.

> Page 53: "Their point of resemblance to each other and their difference from so many American women, lay in the fact that they were all happy to exist in a man's world. They preserved their individuality through men and not by opposition to them. They would all three have made alternatively good courtesans or good wives not by the accident of birth but through the greatest accident of finding their man or not finding him."

That is, I think, a profound and simple philosophic statement. I like it.

30 September 1967, Saturday Morning

It's 6:20 and this morning is pay call. The last regular pay call I'll have in the Army, the last time I'll have to salute and say, "Sir, Specialist reports for pay." I've dreaded that thing every month since I entered the Army. And now I can see an end to it. The next time I get paid will be in Oakland by a pay clerk.

Time for formation.

6:30 p.m.

I've spent all afternoon sleeping, so I'm rested and ready for an evening reading *Tender is the Night*. I'm on page 164 and discovered today that the book is really about perverse sex, something I'd only felt indirectly before. Also I found out what Mrs. McKisco saw in the bathroom, because Rosemary saw the same. The episode about the negro who died in Rosemary's bed was an interesting handling of race—something that Hemingway didn't ever interest himself in.

The *Tender is the Night* I'm reading starts with Rosemary on the beach. A good start. He does the same in *Gatsby*; I mean specifically we gradually become aware of the main character, seeing him first around the edges before he's directly presented to us.

Today I received my last regular Army pay. Roy Acuff just came on. "Local pool room burned down, 400 boys left homeless." Ha Ha. Old Roy is singing

"Fraulein." He's too much. Grandpa Jones just came on the TV, a yodeling fool.

Over here they'll develop any kind of pictures that we take. Yes, we soldiers are an evil bunch. I don't care what anybody says.

Cousin Brucie just came on FM radio. What a D.J. The original screamer. I'm going to read now. I'll write more in the morning before I leave for work.

I just returned from a cold shower and feel alert and clean. Now I'm going to watch "Lost in Space."

1 October 1967, Sunday Morning

It's 6:45, and the first day of the month I get out. That makes me feel short, at least 'til I get used to the idea of it being October. This morning at work I'll try to read *Tender is the Night,* if no one has ideas about me working.

Time to go to work.

6:35 p.m.

I'm going to eat popcorn for a while and write more later.

2 October 1967, Monday Morning

It's 5:45 and I woke up this morning with popcorn on my breath. I dreamt about a record by Bob Dylan last night, an old folk-type song, but the thing had three sides—it really did. I finished

Tender is the Night yesterday at work. I can't understand why Fitzgerald's novels are usually viewed as period piece novels. His people aren't period piece people, but more real than any I've encountered lately. *Tender is the Night* is a much more complex novel than *Gatsby*. He tries to grapple with truths about the relationship of husband and wife that most writers never even thought about. The writing gets sloppy occasionally, but the first person section in which Nicolle talks is a fine piece of writing. Reminds me of a Styron thing in which the girl talks her piece.

Yesterday Lt. Col. Rollins' replacement came in. I don't know if he'll be in the office today or not, but he's a great big fat fellow, Rollins says. Rollins will be out of the office on an investigation today, and Kathy will be on her Monday sick call. I'll be glad to be out of an office—a nice job as a meter-reader would surely be pleasant.

Somewhere above I ate breakfast. Now it's time for formation, at which time we'll have to go police around the mess hall. Goody Gumdrop.

9:30 p.m.

Today I got back some slides I took in Bien Hoa. The first really good slides I've taken. Of the twenty, three or four are good, and two of them would make anybody comment, look again, and react to them. They aren't taken too professionally. I've got the camera turned the wrong way, but the lighting and all that is fine. No slides of the sergeant major skulking. Maybe those will be in the next batch.

Three (in a row) by Donovan are playing. "Catch
the Wind" is playing now. It must be one of the
finest love songs of today. Now "There is no
Mountain" is playing. Today I did nothing all day
except read Robert Penn Warren's Flood—at my
desk, feet on my desk, red clay from boots on my
desk.

Today Lt. Col. Hawk entered our office. He's a
fat, hearty, boyish fellow, a good man.

Major Tief returned from R&R today. On R&R
he had a time. First off, before leaving country, he
found out on a Sunday he needed a passport for
Penang. He was to leave early on a Monday, so on
Sunday he called Ambassador Ellsworth Bunker at
his home, and Bunker got him a counsellor to get
him a passport. Also Tief lost his suitcase (left it
sitting at Tan Son Nhut) and while in Penang got
$170 lifted from his wallet. The story he gave
Bunker to get that passport was masterful. Major
Tief is a gifted con man. If he weren't a drunk he'd
have it made. That's a big if, as they say.

As soon as Major Tief got into the office he
jumped me about my long hair curling about my
ears, not wearing my dogtags, not carrying a
Geneva Convention card, etc. I just grinned at him
and kept reading Flood.

Our office is jammed with people, desks, two
lieutenant colonels, a major, a colonel, and two
clerks, all within a couple feet of each other. Lt.
Col. Rollins just said, "If you think his hair is long
you should see his replacement's." Don's hair is
long, long. Major Tief said, "Well, I've been over-
ruled again." But he felt no loss, I know.

"Give me a ticket for an aeroplane . . ." is on. I
like the line and the way he says it. One line can

make a hit, and frequently does. Time to go to bed.

3 October 1967, Tuesday, 5:40 a.m.

It's morning and I'm sitting on my bunk again, listening to Country Corner and writing. Soon this will all be at an end and I'll not be up at this hour, nor writing like this, I'm sure. This is the last piece of paper in this steno pad, so I'll have to procure another one somewhere. Today I plan to go to the dentist to see if he can find a few teeth he can salvage. ("The teeth are fine, but the gums will have to come out.") Time to go to breakfast.

9:05 p.m.

I'm watching the Steve Allen Show. Steve and Jayne are singing a duet. Oh what a lovely day while the elements run amuck. Lou Rawls is a guest. He's not come on tonight. Today at work I did nothing except read. One fine spy novel and something called *Stud on the Loose,* or such like. It was written in 1937 and in one scene there is a picture of Taft on the piano.

Rawls is doing "Windy City." Much later, Steve Allen, Jayne, Louie Nye, Tim Conway, et al. just did a musical werewolf thing that was funny—corny funny.

Time for me to shower. I've not bothered for a couple of days due to the cold weather, but I truly must bother tonight.

Oh yeah, I went to the dentist today. He said I have one tiny cavity. I guess I'll go in Monday and get it filled. After immersing my teeth in Coke for two years I expected the worst. My teeth need cleaning too, but they won't do that. Time yet for a shower.

I'm just back from an icy shower and now to bed.

4 October 1967, Wednesday Morning

It's 5:30 and I am listening to "Wall to Wall Heartaches" and that's a lot of heartache. Last night I packed most of my books and all of my records and other odds and ends and will send them off sometime in the next few days. Almost time for formation.

9:00 p.m.

The day was a bit busier but I didn't do much. Typed five or six endorsements. Mostly I just read Pedigree by Simenon, or goofed around. Tomorrow I'm going to take my camera to the office and immortalize the mamasans and the other folks on celluloid.

That old folk ballad "Louie, Louie" just ended and now Donovan is stumbling through that "Mountain" thing. When it's over it'll run through my mind for hours.

I just got a Wink and I'm drinking the thing and listening to that Beatles song that should be everyone's keynote for a new life— "We Can Work it Out." ". . . Life is very short and there's no time for fussing and fighting, my friend . . ." No, my friend, there isn't any time. These last thirteen months

have convinced me of that. I always need convincing
of everything. Well, I've been convinced.

I'm going to piss and will do more in the
morning.

5 October 1967, Thursday Morning

Today I get off work at 5:00 because I have CQ
again tonight. That means I'll be off work all day
tomorrow. Which is fine with me. I've got plenty to
read. I'm getting tired of reading and writing,
though. I've had enough of that stuff, at least in the
vacuum that this place is.

> *"Down in the meadow*
>   *where the green grass grows,*
> *There sat Jimmy*
>   *with a marble up his nose."*
>   *— Folk Saying*

10:00 p.m.

I'm sitting in the orderly room performing my
CQ duties, and right now the Four Tops are singing
that fine song "I can't help myself, I love you and
nobody else." Better known as "Sugar Pie Honey
Bunch."

This fucking typewriter is a monster. I prefer
my Adler, although that thing is just one step from
the junk heap. That's were it will go when I leave
country. I'm leaving soon, actually. My hair is about
as long as it can get in my present position. I'd feel
strange wearing short hair in such cool weather. I
hope I'll have a sheepskin coat to wear, too.

This afternoon I went to several PXs, but just as a spectator as I have no money. I'll be off all day tomorrow, but anticipate it with no great pleasure as there is nothing I really want to do, whether it be reading or whatever. I'd like to take some pictures, but I'd rather be taking them in Seattle.

I've been devouring novels all day and my eyes are in very sorry shape. By morning I'll probably be able to focus on nothing. I'm about half way into a novel called *The Case of the Murdered Madame* by Henry Kane, and it doesn't seem too fine. I'm ruined for reading bad mysteries by the novels of Simenon, and L'Amour has made it impossible to appreciate bogus oaters. So there I am, with sensibilities and nothing with which to feed them. Ah well, soon I'll be fed to the full.

Woody Guthrie got an obit in *Stars and Stripes,* but it was only an anticlimax as we'd all bid him good-bye a long time ago. A fine writer, especially in his novel-type attempts, and very similar to others who've gotten much more attention. The guy who wrote *Somebody in Boots,* for instance.

It's raining outside right now. Even though this is allegedly the dry season. But drip drip drip.

Later:

It's 2:00 a.m. and I'm listening to the second game of the World Series. Anyhow, it's on the radio and I've got it on, although I'd prefer to listen to music. But there isn't any.

It's going to be a long night, I think, and in the morning I'll sleep the sleep of the innocent. I had a headache earlier, but it seems to have wandered off somewhere.

"All you need is love
Love is all you need."

6 October 1967, Friday, 8:20 p.m.

The old Beatles are singing that fine song. I spent the day in bed recovering from an arduous night as CQ, of which I slept about four hours.

Today I got my port call. I report to 90th Replacement on 22 October 1967 at 20:00 hours (8:00 p.m.). I leave on a flight at 0801 hours (8:00 a.m.) on 23 October. I'll get to Oakland the morning of 23 October and spend twelve to twenty-four hours processing, so I'll be in Seattle the 24th, most likely. That's not bad as I could have done much worse. Only sixteen days left in-country.

Today I got back a roll of 36 black and white pictures I shot in Bien Hoa. 38 came out. No pictures of the sergeant major. Ain't that peculiar? It's possible to get extra pictures sometimes. The pictures were fine, focus and all. Some of them could have been selected better, but I'm improving. The black and whites look so much more professional than the slides. My PetriFlex V-6 pleases me. I wasn't so sure about it at first, but now that I've learned to use it, I think I'll get some attachments for it. The September *Playboy* has an ad for the exact one I've got, so they must still be in production or they'd not hardly bother with an ad in *Playboy,* now would they.

I'm drinking a Miller High Life out of a rusty old can as I've got no Cokes. But soon I'll be drinking Rainier Ale out of those green bottles.

I guess I'll watch Matt Dillon for a while and write more tomorrow morning.

7 October 1967, Saturday Morning

It's 5:40 and big band (ugh) music on the radio signals the fact that it's Saturday, otherwise I'd never know it. Big band music is the most overrated shit (a damned sacred cow) that is cherished by those who should know better. "Chattanooga Choo Choo, why don't you choo choo me home?" Insipid. A good question, though. Now the D.J. is debating Benny Goodman's ability on the clarinet and Glen Miller's ability on trombone—mostly the latter. How many angels can dance on the head of a pin? It depends on the size of their feet and how big the pin is.

Time to go to breakfast. I've got a full work day ahead of me although I've tomorrow off. I hope I'm not required to do anything today. I don't feel up to any work. I'm too short.

8 October 1967, Sunday, 7:25 p.m.

Today Charlie and I went downtown Bien Hoa and took a few pictures. It failed to lift my spirits, however. The whole Vietnamese scene depresses me. We caught no glimpse of the sergeant major, distant or otherwise.

This morning I was awakened at 8:00 as the sergeant major wanted me to go to work and unlock my desk, as he couldn't find the second key to my desk. He accused me of having it, which was untrue. Tomorrow I'll give him a piece of my mind. I'll be thrilled to see the end of that awful man.

A replacement finally arrived, a SP5 who had the same teachers at Ft. Ben as I.

9 October 1967, Monday, 5:35 a.m.

Here it is morning and I feel like most people must feel at this time of the day, except I've got the beginnings of a cold, too. Ah well, a thousand years from now who'll remember these days? (Me.) I guess I'll shave now.

Well, I'm back and my neck aches. It may be because I didn't go to sleep last night 'til 12:00 and got up at 5:00 this morning.

Time for breakfast.

8:00 p.m.

Today I sent my hold baggage. It will arrive much later than I myself will, although it still seems a mighty long time. I should be in Seattle the 24th, barring holdups.

I surely wish I had someone's soft, sweet attention this evening as I'm really a sickie and feeling mighty sorry for myself, as I always do when I'm sick. I have all the symptoms of a classic cold. Hot lemonade, a hot bath, and two sweet breasts pressed to my face would revive me completely, or I'd die happy.

My replacement, Don, moved into my office today, displacing Kathy. Don took right over. I'll not be doing much the next few days—except coughing and snorting.

I'm going to sleep now.

11 October 1967, Wednesday Morning

It's 5:45. I didn't sleep well last night, but I feel pretty good this morning, considering. I guess I'll wander up to the mess hall.

7:55 p.m.

Today was one of those days unmitigated by any tangible pleasures. One alarm after another all day. I hope I get out of this command with a few nerves unruint and my temper not completely shot. Tomorrow will be especially nasty. We start off with a flu shot at 5:15 a.m. I tried to get the sergeant major to find a way to get me out of the shot because I'm short, but he just threw up his hands. He's such a comfort. Don (my replacement) will be busy all day doing the quarterly report. I'll type my usual slow and erratic speed and just let the shit pile up.

The flu shot will probably put me under, with the cold I've got and as weak, sickly, etc. as I am. But unflinchingly, like a man, I'll take my punishment. Whimper whimper.

13 October 1967, Friday, 9:00 p.m.

I've already recovered from my flu shot of yester morn, and I think my cold is also on the wane.

Today wasn't especially unlucky, but just another shitty day. One crummy thing after another, all

day. And I know who was behind them. He hopes
I'll crack up before I leave RVN. Well, I'll fool him!
I hope. I feel on the edge of sanity, slipping fast.

Tomorrow I work only half day and I have
Sunday off, which will be a drag as I'm going to sit
in the barracks all day. Bien Hoa will never see my
hatchet face nor hear my sweet voice again. A new
big PX just opened up today right near my barracks. If I had some money I'd spend it, so I guess
it's just as well that I'm broke, except for $10.

Tonight riding the bus back from work, two
cruds behind me were discussing Seattle and the
lousy weather there (alleged rain). I said bull shit,
and asked them what they were talking about. They
said they'd been at Ft. Lewis. I tried to explain to
them that the weather differs, and it was almost
settled in a fist fight. My temper has been very
short lately. The period of my extension has been
the hardest part of my tour over here, and I can
almost daily see my supply of good humor and high
spirits depleting. If I had it to do over again, I
doubt whether I'd extend. The strain of these extra
42 days isn't really a thing I'd be able to go through
again.

"Give me a ticket for an airplane . . . I don't care
how much I got to spend . . . But I got to get back to
my baby . . ." now playing. A fine song. But I'm sure
that once I'm home I'll quickly forget these last
weeks here and I'll be glad to have avoided three
months of Stateside service. But these 42 days here
have been the most emotionally exhausting of all.
Not the work load, just the torment of the place,
expecially being butted up against my nemesis from
Italy, Sergeant Major Smith. And waiting for the
other shoe to drop. It seems unlikely anything of

moment will transpire at this late date. Ah well, I
guess I'll make it. Time will tell, as they say. I'm
off to sleep now.

15 October 1967, Sunday, 9:00 p.m.

I'm getting short. I feel it in my bones. Today I
spent all day on my bunk, reading or messing with
my camera. I read a spy novel, *The Man From
Pansie.* The spy's thing is that he's a pretended
homosexual. Also I bought a book *Traditional Cul-
ture and the Impact of Technological Change.* Of
course all of Vietnam is an open air textbook in
this subject. Also today I listened to my radio on
shortwave much of the day—Radio Ceylon, Voice of
America, and a bunch of unidentified others. Our
area here in the barracks looks like a kitchen
midden after a weekend of eating and drinking with
no mamasan to carry off the trash.

Today we got a letter from old Dead Head Ed.
His girl didn't wait for him but was making it with
his best friend, so she gave him back the million
dollars worth of junk he'd given her, and he left
Kalispell, Montana, and is now back in San Luis
Obispo attending Cal Poly again. I hope he can get
up to Seattle occasionally when I get home. Old Ed
said that she said she'd not told him about it
because he was in Vietnam and all. Kinda funny—
and sad.

This week I'll be sending a bunch of junk back
home through the mail—boots, odds and ends, stuff
I'll not want to carry. I'm not leaving with any
baggage—none. Nothing I've got is worth wearing
again. I'll have to buy all new socks and underwear

when I get home. The stuff is either rotting or permeated with fungi. And that ain't good.

Tomorrow is going to be another one of those days. Lt. Col. Rollins spent all day today grinding out letters and endorsements that Don and I will have to type. On the 22nd I report to 90th and I leave at 0800 on the 24th, that morning, so I should have the 20th and 21st off to clear this crummy place. So Thursday *should* be my last day in the office, but it probably won't be.

I'll be presented with my green hornet this week (the Army Commendation Medal—John Brown went off to war . . .). Also this week I'll throw my going-away beer blast. Tradition must be observed.

Last night I went to sleep at 8:30 and slept 'til 10:30 this morning. I'm not tired especially, as I did nothing all day. Nothing exhausting, that is. Though Saturday I walked the million miles to Chase Manhattan and cashed a $10 check someone sent me.

Time to read a bit more of something. I'll write something in the morning.

16 October 1967, Monday Morning

It's 5:45, my last Monday in country, unless I count the little bit of next Monday morning before I leave. I forgot to mention that Saturday at the PX I saw a fellow I went through basic with—the first one I've seen in more than thirteen months in country. He was a SP5. He's a kid from Seattle. Vernon. Ah, shades of the past. Time for breakfast.

"It's the same old song,
But with a different meaning,
Since you've been gone . . ."
— Four Tops

8:45 p.m.

The Four Tops are singing that fine song of loss and the effect of it.

Today was another day, busy and crammed with work. At least it makes the time go by swiftly. Next Monday at this time I could be out of the Army, or almost anyhow.

I still haven't sent any junk in the mail. I'll have to start soon. I can hardly carry the stuff I've got left.

Tomorrow I hope to go on a chopper ride to take a few pictures. Should only last a few minutes.

Today Col. Ebby asked me if I wanted him to write a letter to anyone telling them how I did here. He takes that junk very, very seriously. If I could ever find a boss like that as a civilian, I'd actually work hard at something for the first time in my lazy life. Col. Ebby responds to my jokes (stories) and personality the way my father never allowed himself to do. Col. Ebby of course has no children, no son, and very much wanted one—as some men do. What a fine thing it is to have a fatherly type such as he respond to a story or a brief bit of nonsense.

For instance, today I said I wasn't really prepared for the Army. My doctor told me the Army would kill me. And when I said, "Will that keep me out?" He said, "Not necessarily." Now, it doesn't seem that funny in the re-telling, but it's all in the timing, pauses, delivery, context, the moment being right, and the audience being a good one. Most "adults" never really had the time for my ostensible frivolities. Oh well, all I'm trying to say is that it was good to be around Col. Ebby for a few months. And it's too bad that I can't communicate as well with my father.

I'm reading a fine thriller called *Night of the Short Knives,* which I think I'll now read for a while. An alert (practice) is expected tonight. Ugh!

17 October 1967, Tuesday Morning, Early

No alert last night, which was no big surprise, especially to me as I was asleep anyhow. The Geezenslaw Brothers are pickin' and singin' right now, "Change of Life." Yes indeed. Now old Merl Haggard is singing "Wine & Roses." And on that note, I guess I'll go. "All my social friends look down their noses, cause I kept the wine and threw away the roses . . ." Yes I did.

9:00 a.m.

Today is the day for my chopper ride. I've been angling for this ride ever since I got in country, and today is the day. Col. Ebby, and before him Lt.Col. Prince, both did everything they could all these months to discourage my flying in a helicopter. Not safe, they said. Well, I'll find out for myself. What can possibly go wrong? Knock on wood. Will write more later.

Later:

I learned Sergeant Major Smith will be going with us on *my* chopper ride. Oh, shit. It'll be hard to have fun with that wet blanket along. But I'll grit my teeth and try.

19 October 1967, Thursday, 10:45 p.m.

I'm back—from the jaws of death. That prosaic chopper ride turned into a real brush with death.

It started off completely normal and uneventful. We departed from the pad adjacent to the office building and headed for the green distance, in the direction of the airstrike I wrote about a while back.

Soon we were flying low over a rice paddy. An ancient papasan in black pajamas was attending to his tasks in the rice paddy, accompanied by his water buffaloes.

Sergeant Major Smith was taking pictures. He missed his photo opportunity and asked to pilot to make another pass at the papasan and his buffaloes, only this time lower and slower, which the pilot proceeded to do.

We waved at the papasan and he waved at us, and then he raised an ancient rifle. It looked like something Abdel Krim used in North Africa. He fired one shot. We all heard it hit the chopper, and rapidly things took a turn for the worse. We suddenly were over the nearby triple-canopied jungle, and the chopper had all the airworthiness of the old-style Maytag wringer washing machine. To say we dropped like a stone wouldn't be accurate, but I can't think of a better cliche. The chopper crashed through the trees and vines, finally coming to rest about twenty feet from the jungle floor.

Because Sergeant Major Smith had been hanging out the chopper door getting his priceless photograph, he was no longer aboard. I didn't notice his going, being occupied in hanging on for dear life myself, but Sergeant Major Smith was gone. I wish I'd seen him depart. Butter could melt in his mouth now. It's hot in the jungle.

I looked at the pilot. He was dead. I saw not a mark on him. Maybe a broken neck. The door gunner was dead too. It looked like he'd caught the single round after it had done its damage to the chopper. It did him no good. My mind was reeling about what to do next. Wait for help? Or get the hell away from the chopper, because V.C. would soon be arriving for the spoils? The papasan was probably a colonel in the local V.C. battalion. What a feather in his cap this would be.

I followed my natural inclination. I lowered myself to the ground, Tarzan-style, and ran. I was convinced that with every tick of my Seiko watch, the V.C. were closer to converging on the chopper.

Shock waves of adrenaline coursed through my system—far more so than when I was typing important letters, even the one for General Westmoreland's signature block. This aspect of the war was very different, and the only practical knowledge I had for dealing with it was Tarzan. His movies were the *only* jungle training I'd had. Run like hell. Put distance between me and trouble. And then go to ground like a dead man—breathe through my ears. So that is what I did. I blundered through the jungle, finding it rather rough going, but determined to get as much distance between me and the chopper as I could.

At some point I tripped on something and fell into a tree of the banyan sort. While I lay there, panting and gasping for breath (as quietly as a winded asthmatic is capable), several short men in black pajamas moved silently past, toward the chopper. I hugged the ground, squinched my eyes shut, and wished I'd listened to Col. Ebby and stayed in the office.

By this time, dark was falling like a heavy black velvet curtain (shades of Edgar Rice Burroughs), even though it was just afternoon by my watch. I spent the night cowering in that tree, and the next day woke up hearing English being spoken.

Special Forces troops, green berets and all, were standing about ten feet from me. I spoke up. They jumped, but their training saved my ass. No shots were fired. An hour later I was back at Long Binh, none the worse for wear. It's a pleasure to deal with thorough-going professionals.

Having seen the war from the jungle side, I'm grateful for having been ensconced safely in an office. Going from reading, and filing the USARV Weekly Downed Aircraft Statistics, to becoming one of those statistics, was a trauma I had not anticipated. It surely brought those mimeographed pages alive for me.

21 October 1967, Saturday

Now to plod through the last details of getting ready to leave, and then . . . get the hell out. To take such a risk while so short—stupid!

Nothing was found of Sergeant Major Smith. I expect he's finally out of my life. This time forever. I was interviewed rather vigorously about the exact happenstance of each of the other military personnel aboard the chopper at the time it was downed. Interrogated is perhaps a better word. They were especially puzzled and concerned about what had happened to Sergeant Major Smith. All I could tell them was what I knew. Eventually they seemed satisfied. Anyway, they ceased their interrogation and my life went on. And if Sergeant Major Smith's life had ceased, that was only right. The incident was clearly precipitated by his greediness for a good photograph of that farmer in his paddy, and perhaps as punishment for his previous sins. I'll never now know what he was up to in Bien Hoa. Maybe just taking pictures of the exotic scenes.

I won't go into all the "I told you so's," and the good-byes, or the ceremony of the Army Commendation Medal. What's the point? It's all an anticlimax now.

23 October 1967, Sunday

I'm at 90th Replacement Battalion, and will be boarding my plane in a few minutes. I made it.

I bid this lovely country and its occupants a final adieu. Thank you all for leaving my precious ass intact!

David A. Willson was born in Seattle on June 30, 1942. He grew up in Yakima, Washington, the Fruitbowl of the Nation, and graduated from the University of Washington in 1964. He served with the USARV Inspector General Section in Vietnam, 1966-1967. He attended Library School at the University of Washington, graduated with an M.L.S. in 1970, and has been employed as a reference librarian at Green River Community College in Auburn, Washington, since 1970. He is now working on a military history of the Willson family, beginning with Lt. Amber Willson who helped take Ticonderoga with Ethan Allen, and ending with Robert R. Willson who served with the Marines at Iwo Jima. Willson is the father of three sons and is hopeful that they will survive their wars as well as the Willsons who went before.

He is the author of two novels, *REMF Diary* and *The REMF Returns*.